Secrets

of

Havenridge

Secrets

of

Havenridge

A novel

Chris Coad Taylor

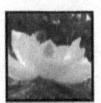

JoHazel Publishing
Land O' Lakes, Florida 34639

JoHazel Publishing
Land O' Lakes, Florida 34639

Printed in the United States
JoHazel ISBN 978-0-9975645-2-5

Acknowledgments

Although it takes a team of people to complete a book, I want to thank two people who especially helped with my revising, *Secrets of Havenridge*, an amazing journey.

Author Tawa Witko helped me by reading and giving me valuable feedback on my revised book. Her words of encouragement and help made my journey an extraordinary one. Like my protagonist who found a friend when she had not expected it, I found Tawa. She is a gracious and giving person. I am pleased to call her a friend.

Sculpture artist Don Haugen. All of Don's sculptures are incredible, that touch and inspire many. I want to thank him for granting me permission to use my photograph of his sculpture of the *Angel of Milledgeville* on the cover of the book.

Links:
https://www.amazon.com/Tawa-M.-Witko/e/B00WH032WE
http://haugensculpture.com/portfolio/angel-of-milledgeville/

Additional books by

Chris Coad Taylor:

The Rainbow Murders
(Amber Novels of Ybor City)

Saffron's Place
(Amber Novels of Ybor City Book 2)
Scheduled for release soon

Finding Jacob
(The Havenridge Mystery Novels- Book 2)

1985

I slept curled up on my bedroom chair, unaware that my life was about to change forever. The rain beats on the window, while the winter night crept into my life and stole my very existence away from me.

***

The evening started when my husband Daniel returned my call. He was eight hundred miles away at a medical conference. It seemed like Daniel was always at a conference somewhere, away from Lily and me.

"You're overreacting, Stephanie." I listened to him lecture to me with his fatherly tone and condescending manner. "Why don't you act like the wife of a doctor, instead of a hysterical mother? You're not new at this. Lily is six years old."

"I'm telling you Daniel, Lily's really sick. Why don't you act like a father and not an 'I know better' doctor and listen to me for once."

"I am listening."

"No, you're not. Listening requires that you consider that someone else could be right. And I'm *not* hysterical. I know how old Lily is; I'm her mother, for goodness' sake. Give me some credit here. When are you going to stop looking down at me, just because I chose motherhood instead of a college diploma?"

"Let's not start this now. I'm tired. It's been a long day and Doctor Clayton and his wife are waiting for me at the bar. My schedule tomorrow is packed and with three more days to teach four thousand surgeons my procedure. I'm not in the mood to debate our daughter's health."

"Oh yes. Go to the back of the line Stephanie," I muttered.

"Stephanie, I can't hear you when you start talking when I'm speaking. What did you say?"

"Daniel, she has a temperature of 102.5. Why can't you do anything? You're a *doctor.*"

"All right! I'll call in some antibiotics, but it will probably need to run its course. Everything can't be perfect, Stephanie. You need to learn that. Children get sick and husbands have to go out of town."

"Stop treating me like a child, or one of your student doctors. I'm a mother and mothers know things."

"And now we're back at the beginning. Yes, my dear, you are smart, in your own way. I need to hang up now so I can call in a prescription for our daughter. Do me a favor, Stephanie, and try to grow up."

I opened my mouth for a rebuttal, but before I could say anything, I heard a click. The discussion was over.

***

Two hours later, after taking Lily out in an unbelievable rainstorm to pick up the medicine at the drugstore, I tucked my daughter into bed. Lily asked in a wheezing voice, "When is Daddy coming home?"

"He has three more days of work."

"Oh. Is Daddy helping other sick children?"

"He's teaching lots of doctors. That way Daddy can help many, many children from all around the world to get better.

But your Daddy told everyone at the conference tonight to wait while he called home so he could take care of his little girl first.

"Daddy called Mr. Nelson at the drug store to tell him which medicine you needed to make you feel better."

"Okay, Mommy. Good night."

"Good night, honey." I bent over and kissed her on the forehead. "You'll feel better tomorrow. I promise."

At her bedroom door, I paused to look at Lily nestled under the pink sheets and comforter. She looked so small under the canopy bed with the pink ruffles that draped the top. Daniel did love her with all his heart, he *was* a good man. Lily had a mommy whose whole life was devoted to her and a father who would die for her, her world was perfect.

I pulled the door closed and walked down the hall to Daniel's and my bedroom. Inside, near the foot of the bed sat the blue velvet chair Daniel bought for me last month as a surprise present for my birthday, never realizing that he missed my actual birthday two months earlier. Nevertheless, he did think of me.

Next to the chair sat a round table with my new book, *Where Are the Children*. I had seen an advertisement about it on television and it intrigued me. I had bought it at the airport after Daniel boarded the plane this week. It was Mary Higgins Clark's debut novel. Reading might help me unwind. Daniel was right. I hover over Lily too much. Children do get sick.

Must I always panic that tragedy is around the next corner?

I picked up the book and sat, turning in the barrel chair, and then I hung my legs over the side. Daniel was caring, that's why he became a doctor. He did love me the best he knew how, like sending the chair when he was the only speaker at the Denver Neo-Surgical World Conference with a visiting group of doctors from Switzerland. Daniel fulfilled all his obligations as *boy genius*, who turned into *doctor extraordinaire*. He tried to be the perfect husband, too. So why couldn't I be happy?

I didn't know the answer, but what I did know was Daniel was wrong. Maybe for the first time in his life, he was wrong. I wasn't unhappy because I chose motherhood. Motherhood was all I ever wanted, and Lily made me happy. She filled me with more happiness than I have ever dreamt was possible.

Being a mother was more important than college, career, or even life itself.

Why can't Daniel see that a child is woven into a mother's soul?

Walking Dead

10 MONTHS LATER.

I woke on the couch in the living room of the small apartment on Bristle Street. The rent was ridiculously high for an efficiency, but it didn't matter. All I needed now was a place to keep the rain off my head. Daniel had offered our house to me in the divorce, but I said no. It was more important for Daniel to have it because it provided a stable environment, which he needed for his life to return to some form of normal. Besides, what would I do in that house all by myself?

I looked over to the table next to my bed. The alarm clock glowed three am. *Two hours of sleep, more than normal.*

It was too late to go for a drive so I decided to make a pot of coffee and wait until time to go to work. Maybe I could wipe the kitchen cabinets out for something to do. I didn't need to do laundry or clean the bathroom. I did that last night.

My insomnia, agitated by the dead feeling inside, made it difficult to function during the day. Still, not being able to sleep, it helped to keep busy. I made coffee. While I waited for it to brew, I pulled a step stool out, climbed up with a rag, and opened the cabinet door. When I pulled down my two plates, my second coffee mug, and the cereal bowl I remembered that I had wiped the cabinet out three nights back.

I stopped and muttered to myself. "There's nothing to do."

After putting the dishes back and putting the step stool away, I poured a cup of coffee. I decided that once it got later,

I'd call work and say that I wouldn't be in today. I'd explain that I was up all night sick. There would be no point going in if I couldn't think straight from lack of sleep.

Nevertheless, I had to get out of the apartment. I would go for a drive. Driving was the only thing that helped me keep my sanity. It took my mind off not having Lily with me anymore.

The file clerk job I had taken three months earlier helped some, but I wondered how long I could keep the job. I figured I would be fired soon because I couldn't remember the office procedures and even after multiple explanations I had been making mistakes. My supervisor had stopped my training out of frustration, no doubt. My life was a mess. I was just as lost as the files I had been given to put away. Everything seemed to go missing near me; it felt as if even my own shadow had disappeared.

North to Georgia

I had never fully understood that whole TGIF thing until recently. In my past life, weekdays were always filled with things to do. I had been Lily's classroom PTA mother, so there was always a class party to plan and projects to organize. No matter how much work piled on me, I still loved every minute, including the spring carnival. It took a half of a year of planning with only four or five volunteers. My life had been full, even having Daniel out of town during most of it I never lacked things to do. The difference between me and the other mothers was that the things that filled my life involved Lily and 6-year-olds. The big difference perhaps was that I rarely had an adult conversation; that is, with Daniel's work demands and traveling.

All that was gone now, my life was changed. It seemed like Daniel and I had reversed the order of things. His days are filled with more demands, and mine, well, my days are filled with nothingness.

***

The last day I spoke to Daniel, we were leaving the courthouse. Daniel paused, apologizing for the way he felt. Said he couldn't help his changed feelings toward me. He tried to feel love, but it was gone. The words, *under the circumstances*, as I recall were the words he used. I still can hear them in my mind. *Stephanie, under the circumstances, it would be better if you don't call.*

He continued, choosing his words carefully as if using the wrong ones might cause a downward spiral that neither of us would be able to recover from.

I wasn't to call him.

Checking in was not needed.

A complete and clean break would be best for everyone involved. Then he wished me well and advised that I should try to make a new life for myself. One without him, or Lily.

A new life, I had thought. *How is that possible?*

Seven years earlier, when I had found out that I was pregnant with Lily, my life made an irreversible change. That single woman that had existed, vanished then. How could I go back? That Stephanie was a memory as elusive as a baby's first cry. Gone forever. A butterfly cannot go back and become a caterpillar again. How could Daniel have suggested that I merely go back to being single?

***

I shook my head to erase the unhappy memories swirling in my head and entered my apartment. Trying to not focus on the past. In a way, Daniel had been right, I needed to find a way to build a new life. What had happened could not be undone.

Glancing at my watch, it showed five minutes after four o'clock. Traffic had been horrific even with leaving work early. I put my purse down on the small table near the door and thumbed through today's mail. Stopping at the large envelope and removing it from the stack, I opened it and unfolded the paper inside. At the top read: Final Order of Dissolution of Marriage.

"Great, just great."

I threw it down on the table and walked over to the portable television set that Daniel had let me take when I moved out and turned it on. An old black and white movie came into focus. A fair-haired woman and man were walking in a cemetery, talking about when they were children. Thunder cracked and the man said something about playing in the cemetery when they were kids.

"They're coming to get you, Barbara."

"Stop it," she responded

A man appeared in the distance, up on the hill. *"Look, there's one of them now."*

Great. *Night of the Living Dead,* just what I needed to calm my nerves and help me sleep. I flipped the television off and went to change my clothes, deciding to go for a drive. It seemed logical, it always helped me relax.

Over this past year, I had followed Daniel's advice and listened to friends and family, who expected me to put the pieces of my life back together. But, I felt like one of those zombies in the movie. I feared that the task of assembling a normal life was impossible. The same as Humpy Dumpy, my life would be broken forever. Maybe the only possible solution would be to move away. Far away from Orlando and make a fresh start. Out of Florida even, maybe somewhere in Georgia.

Georgia had been where I had found myself often driving on the nights when I couldn't sleep. After hours of driving, I would cross into Georgia. The problem was that I didn't have enough time, or the energy to drive back to Orlando for work the next day. The next day, I would arrive late, my co-workers' disapproving looks would bore into me when I'd walk into the office in the same clothes from the day before. The louder than normal whispers as I passed by were ugly. People at work hated me. My boss remained outwardly neutral, as he systemically called me in to "have a talk" about my tardiness and my work performance, documenting each warning. Since I had already gone passed the 90-day trial period, he couldn't justify outright firing me. I understood that we were dancing-the-dance until he had written up enough warnings to justify firing me. My time was running out.

Therefore, my decision wasn't that hard to make: Tonight on my drive I would look for a new town to move to and to make a new start. *If I find something, maybe I'll stay longer than the weekend and call in sick on Monday and Tuesday.*

There was nothing to keep me in Orlando. Friends were gone. Everyone hated me, except for my brother. Moving would be good all the way around. Of course, Steve would argue about my decision to move. Poor Steve, he tried so hard to help me, but it wasn't fair to let my troubles keep weighing my baby brother down. He called every night. Except for his calls and going to work, I lived a life of isolation. Everything that once surrounded me had fallen away, leaving me in hollowness.

It's been a year since . . . "It's time for a new beginning," I said out loud. "I need to put my old life behind me."

Night Drives

I had no particular destination in mind other than Georgia. My plan was to drive until I had to surrender to sleep. I wasn't sure how many hours I had driven but it was dark, now. On an impulse after crossing the Florida-Georgia state line, I had left the main highway. I was exhausted. I had pushed myself too far.

The stars were out and the noise of the highway had fallen away many miles back. The last sign I passed said 55 mph. I had no idea where I was or if I was even heading toward a town. Maybe my impulse decision to take a countryside scenic route hadn't been such a good idea.

The road snaked endlessly with the full moon lighting my way. If not for my fatigue, I would have enjoyed the solitude and peacefulness of the night. Age-old trees, majestic in size, cast shadows on the road as it bent to the right, then left. Not long after, I noticed the road had straightened out and was going toward a hill, straight ahead on the horizon. Once I got near the top, about a half-mile ahead, there appeared the glimmer of lights of a small town.

I continued toward the lights. About ten minutes later, I entered a town. Its shape formed a square of streets lined with stores, with a distinguishing building in the center. The red brick building spotlighted in the center of the square was adorned with white pillars and roughly twenty steps that led up to tall double doors. Above the doors, a sign read City Hall. An image popped into my head of an enormous Christmas tree on the front lawn, complete with carolers in bright red sweaters.

The exclusion of Main Street seemed to be the only visible difference between this quaint town somewhere in Georgia and Mayberry, U.S.A.

Oh, perfect! I've found City Hall, but what city am I in?

Havenridge

After driving around the square twice, I figured the entire collection of stores probably could be seen on a brisk twenty-minute walk. For a little town, it had a good variety of shops. Among some of those was a gift shop, one general store, and a barbershop with the cliché red and white striped pole out front. Next to the front door, under the barber pole sat a bench. I almost could picture Floyd and Andy Griffith sitting there.

The town looked like a Norman Rockwell painting. I could not believe a town like this still existed in 1986.

Many of the stores had already closed. To add to my exhaustion, frustration kicked in when I realized that this one-horse town must shut down at sunset. I scanned the dark store windows, hoping to see a light or any flicker of activity.

There... the general store has lights on. It must be open. I didn't care where I was, just as long as I could be pointed in the direction of a motel. I couldn't push myself to drive any further.

A quick look in the rearview mirror before opening the car door and I realized that I was quite a sight. Before I left home, I had changed into my favorite sky-blue pants with an elastic waistband. They were comfortable, but wouldn't win any fashion awards. The pants still wore remnants of yellow and orange stains from when I painted the kitchen before Lily's last birthday party. Despite their messy appearance, I couldn't part

13

with them. The T-shirt was one I purchased at a fundraiser for an aquarium's grand opening. The underwater scene on the front sported an array of fish in shades of blue; navy, turquoise, teal, but none quite matched the sky-blue color of my pants. Stylish apparel hadn't been on my mind when I threw on the abomination of mismatched colors since I hadn't planned to see anyone tonight. My only thought had been to drive and *escape from people*. Now, that thought seemed as ill-planned as my, *move away and everything will be better* scheme.

I wished now that I had at least combed my hair before leaving so that I wouldn't look like a nut case who had just escaped the funny farm. It was strange that I cared about my appearance, here, in a town I'd never been to and most likely would never come to again.

"Stephanie Oliver, you have to get a grip on your life," I spoke out loud, half under my breath, as I walked to the only opened store. Continuing scolding myself like an insane person, I mumbled, "You're only thirty-five years old, there are years ahead of you. Daniel has moved on, you need to start caring about life again."

In the last few weeks, I had been having these pep talks daily, but nothing seemed to work. My loneliness was suffocating me. Still, I just didn't care. I ran my fingers through my tangle of hair. I had always hated the natural mousey brown color. It had been months since I'd been to the beauty salon. Lily loved it when I came home with my hair heavily frosted blonde. She used to say I looked like Blondie and she would shriek, "Sing Heart of Glass, Mommy!"

I had stopped going to the salon after losing Lily. Besides, every time I went to the salon all the old bittys there would shoot me judgmental looks then would start whispering and pointing at me.

The sight of women whispering in beauty salons is a rare scene. Because a beauty salon is somewhat like sacred ground and women seem to speak about anything, never keeping secrets. Much like men when speaking freely with bartenders. When talking while under a hairdryer, it is nearly impossible to realize exactly how loud you're speaking. Women tend to yell whatever gossip they're secretly divulging. It is all 'out in the open' in salons, whether it's planned that way or not.

***

Tuesday used to be my regular hair appointment day. Everyone spoke in whispers after *that Tuesday*. It was the last Tuesday I went to get my hair done.

I sat there wanting to disappear as I watched a hairstylist hurry over to those two old bats under the dryers. She tried to alert them that everyone could hear them.

The woman's voice bellowed over the dryers. "There's that Oliver woman getting her hair highlighted. She doesn't deserve to live after the way she took care of her daughter. She's a doctor's wife, you know. Some people don't deserve to be a parent."

***

I stopped walking, frozen as I viewed the scene in my mind. It would be etched there forever. Tears trickled down my cheeks. Blinking back to reality, I wiped my face.

"That was a long time ago, Stephanie. Those old bittys are a good reason to move away." I said, hoping to force myself to return to the present.

I started walking fast, knowing that if I didn't hurry the only store open would close and I would be sleeping in my car. After all, I was lost somewhere in Georgia and needed to focus.

One more wipe of my eyes, I needed to be alert and without wet, teary eyes so I could speak intelligently as I asked for directions to the nearest motel. As I hurried toward the store, I felt a sudden calmness flow over me. It seemed as if I had stepped back in time to the comfort of this small town. A blanket of tranquility wrapped around me, a feeling I thought had been lost forever for me.

How can this modest little community I don't even know the name of, be so . . . enchanted?

Sarah

Upon entering the general store, I received polite greetings from some shoppers along with curious looks as they wandered about the store. I felt the attention was not about my appearance, but seemed more as if I had walked into the store with two heads.

"Hi, I'm Sarah," said a pretty woman behind the counter. "I'm the owner of the store. How can I help you?"

"I'm looking for a motel. I've been on the road for some time. To be honest, I'm lost. I don't even know what town I'm in."

"You're in Havenridge."

Havenridge. At least I have the name of where I am. Maybe that means I'm really not lost.

As most of the customers piled out of the store, each paused to take one last hard look at me. After a small exchange of information with Sarah, I asked why I got the strange looks and stares from people.

She blushed and lowered her voice as if not wanting to be heard by the two remaining customers lingering behind. "Havenridge is very small-townish."

The man and woman to our right appeared to be straining to listen in on our conversation. "In the eyes of people who live in Havenridge," Sarah whispered, "it's just not commonplace to

17

see a young woman traveling alone at night. And then, it's taboo for her to ask for directions to . . ." she paused, glancing at the two people who still were craning their necks to hear. Sarah pulled her hand up to cover her mouth, leaned forward, and said, "*a motel.*"

"That's ridiculous," I said in a normal voice. The man grabbed the woman's arm and pulled her out of the store without looking back.

Sarah giggled and replied, "Yeah, well people around here are a little set in their ways. Are you traveling to visit someone around here?"

"No, I don't know anyone. I just got bored with the highway and thought it would be nice to take the less-traveled road. Sundown snuck up on me and in the dark, everything looks the same. I think I've been driving in circles."

"Oh, that's easy to do in these back roads, especially at night," she said. "I'm sorry, but this town doesn't have a motel. That's why I figured you must have known someone around here since there are only two exits that bring you through town. Normally people stop here for only a few hours to do a little shopping, or maybe for something to eat on their way to somewhere else. There's not enough here to keep them here overnight unless they're coming to visit relatives. In that case, they stay with their families."

A town without a motel? Now I must have stepped into a Norman Rockwell painting.

A headache was forming and I rubbed my forehead, trying to assess the situation. If I loaded up with some soda and cookies that probably would keep me awake with the sugar high. At least, long enough to drive to the next town.

The blond woman behind the counter looked concerned. "You look tired. Have you been on the road long?"

"Yes, I really should've stopped for the night an hour ago. That's when I decided to leave the highway. I don't want to fall asleep driving. Is the next town close? Can you give me directions?"

She picked up the phone, I thought she was going to dial directory assistance to get the number of a hotel for me so I could call ahead to reserve a room.

She said as she dialed, "You can't drive, you're too tired and it's too dark. You'll get lost again. I'll call Betsy."

"What? . . . Who?" This was crazy. Mayberry was turning into a Twilight Zone episode.

"Betsy and Joe Wilcox. They used to rent out a room to Eric Trenton a few years back. That is until he and Marcy Bass got married and bought the Pierson's' house on Primrose Road."

Without missing a beat, or even pausing to take a breath, she continued explaining. "I'm sure Betsy would be more than happy to have you stay with them."

"Oh no. That's all right. I can drive to the next town," I said weakly. I didn't truly want to stay at a home of someone I didn't know but I felt my eyes growing heavier. It was getting late and I was too tired to argue or even think straight.

Sarah squealed, "Good!" "I knew you wouldn't mind," she said into the phone. "I'll give her directions to your house."

Sarah spoke on the phone a few more minutes before saying goodbye. As she set the phone in its cradle, she said, "It's all taken care of. Betsy is putting fresh sheets on the bed. You're going to love her. She's a dear."

"Uh, okay. Thank you," I said pushing at my temples to lessen the throbbing in my head.

That was how I found Havenridge. Or, should I say, how Havenridge found me.

Betsy

How I made it to Betsy's house I'm not sure, because I kept nodding off while driving. The light on a veranda of a distant house shot through the darkness of night, beckoning to me. I turned toward it and followed its light, like a ship in distress on a stormy night, reaching out to a beam of light cast from a welcoming lighthouse.

A young woman, appearing to be in her mid-thirties, was sitting in a porch chair near hanging baskets of flowers. I would soon learn that it was Betsy Wilcox, wife of Joe, and Sarah's best friend.

I climbed out of the car and grabbed my small cosmetic case that had all overnight essentials necessary for a one-night stay. Inside were pajamas, a hairbrush, my toothbrush, clean underwear, and makeup.

Betsy stood and hurried to me, meeting me at the bottom of the front steps. "Did you find the house okay? It's only ten minutes from the shop but it seemed to be a while since Sarah called."

"Yes, Sarah was a great help but I think I might have made a wrong turn coming here. When I saw your light, I figured this was it."

Betsy insisted on carrying my case. She put her arm around my shoulder with a warm, gentle squeeze and said, "Well, I'm so glad you're here. Joe's in the kitchen fixing you a nice cup of tea."

Betsy's hair was short and brown. She instantly made me feel welcomed, as if I belonged there, like a dear old friend. She had big eyes, which dominated her face. Not in a way of being out of proportion, but they were noticeably the prettiest feature of her natural beauty. A beauty that was more than surface.

She seemed to radiate a perfection that came from within that you couldn't help but take notice. And her blue eyes were not just captivating. They had an old-soul look in them.

We entered the kitchen where a man in a plaid shirt and jeans stood in front of a big farm sink with his back toward us.

"Joe, she's here. This is Stephanie."

He shut the running water off, grabbed a towel, and dried his hands. He had jet-black hair and smiled with an impish half-grin that was enhanced by one dimple at the corner of his mouth. If I had been a teenager, I would have described him as a hunk. He probably was the kind of guy who could've done anything in school and gotten away with it by melting you with his smile and innocent looks. He was a perfect match for Betsy's beauty.

I thought that they probably had been prom king and queen in school with looks like that. Although Betsy's dress was conservative, she had a richer look that came from a person with a sense of fashion.

"Hello, Stephanie. I understand that you've had a long night." He pulled a chair out for me and I sat. There were what appeared to be fine bone china teacups and saucers sitting waiting for us. Three to be exact.

Joe moved over to the stove and grabbed a teakettle, bringing it to the table and sat down. Betsy poured the hot water into a flowered china teapot. She said that she hoped I like Peachberry Jasmine tea.

Bone china and Peachberry Jasmine tea in the middle of farm country seemed strangely out of place. But then, so did a beautiful woman wearing understated clothes that visibly were neither plain nor homemade. It all seemed odd. Her dress had a stylish flair and sophistication to it. Although Betsy didn't appear to acknowledge her beauty or gracefulness by 'putting on airs,' as my mother used to say the rich girls did at my high school when I was a teenager.

Betsy seemed to show no importance to the china on the table nor to her clothing. It was as if her dress choice was only a mere necessity of daily living, and what to wear depended only on what was the first thing she pulled out of the closet in the morning.

"I'm sorry to impose on you both," I said. "Please don't feel you need to entertain me."

Joe burst out laughing. "Impose? Entertain you? Stephanie, it's obvious you know nothing about my wife. She wouldn't know how *not* to treat someone in our home as a guest. She'll mother you to death if you let her. And she'll be tickled pink doing it."

He pushed his chair out, stood, and bent down, and gave Betsy a kiss on the cheek. "That being said, ladies, I'm going to take this opportunity to bid you both a good night. I've done my duty boiling the water for tea and setting the table. Stephanie, that plate in the middle has Betsy's homemade ginger snap cookies. The best ever and they go great with the Peachberry Jasmine tea. I'm going to bed. Five a.m. comes way too quickly and I have a field to tend to in the morning. Good night, ladies. Enjoy yourselves."

Joe seemed young, probably in his thirties like Betsy. However, they related to each other differently than most couples their age. I could feel the connection they had and the unspoken devotion. There was an aura about them that was so strong, which usually comes when a married couple has been together for fifty or sixty years.

After that weekend, I found myself drawn to Havenridge. I made regular trips, staying with Joe and Betsy. Despite the closeness of their age to my own, they radiated deeper wisdom that gave me a feeling of being in the presence of elders. Still, I didn't speak of important moral issues with Betsy or any serious topics. Our talks consisted more about chitchat regarding the people of the town.

I'm ashamed to say, I acquired a good bit of the weekly gossip of the Havenridge residents by taking advantage of Betsy's obvious boredom that came from being the wife of a farmer. It turned out to be a great escape for me. Especially since Betsy seemed more than comfortable being the center of the conversation, she hardly ever asked me questions about myself. And I preferred to keep it that way.

As Betsy shared stories about town bake sales, Fourth-of-July festivals, and the teenagers from the school's marching band that played in the town gazebo, I grew to love everything I heard about this cozy community. Maybe there had been a reason for losing my way on that night.

In my journey, I stumbled onto a hidden treasure where the birds sang and the children still played outside after the sun went down. Havenridge was a jewel found right out in the open. My jewel, a sparkling diamond, surrounded by the fast pace of twentieth-century cities, flourishing in the sweet-smelling air of old-time Georgia.

I came to the conclusion that Havenridge would give me the seclusion needed to bury my past and make a fresh start.

My New Life

I moved in early springtime. It felt very poignant because springtime in the garden is when life starts over—new and fresh.

My brother, Steve, wasn't happy about my plans to move. He said he worried about me being a woman alone and argued I would be hours away from his help. I knew my mental state troubled him. What frightened me the most was that Steve knew me better than anyone in the world. I needed to distance myself from him. My brother saw me as if I were one of Betsy's fragile china teacups. I knew that he wanted to keep me close so he could protect me from *breaking,* again.

Steve frantically used logic to persuade me not to move. "I understand, Steph. You need to make a fresh start. But you can do that here where you have support from the people who love you. Remember, you're not really alone."

I didn't answer him. Except for him, there weren't any "people who loved me" in Orlando. Steve couldn't see the truth. My silence stopped any possible debate. I suppose he realized my mind was made up because his eyes took on the sadness of defeat.

Of course, my baby brother still loved me. His love was unconditional. Steve ached for anyone in pain. He had a gentle heart and the tenderness of an angel, even had the looks of one, too. Honey-blonde hair and soft blue eyes. If anyone's eyes could be called "the windows to the soul," his could.

Our mother died five years earlier, so I knew my brother understood the struggle of loss. However, nothing can compare to the emptiness in a mother's heart when she cannot see her child grow up, or never be able to hold her again. Living in Orlando only gave me a feeling of numbness.

To keep my sanity, I had to move and become someone else. I needed to be somewhere, anywhere, that I could walk in a neighborhood without judging eyes following me. Somewhere, I could eventually find peace from what I did.

***

A FEW MONTHS BEFORE MY MOVE

Betsy and I were visiting on her front porch. She started by saying, "Homes in Havenridge don't go up for sale very often. Families around here are close-knit and don't move away. There are folks here who were born in the same house where their parents were born. In fact, this house was my parent's home."

I had never known any adult who was living in their childhood home. People in Florida, at least the part where I was from, were mostly transplanted Northerners who came down for work or to retire.

"You've never lived anywhere else?" I asked.

"Oh yes, I went to college. Joe had been accepted at the same university the year before on a football scholarship. I lived in an apartment near the campus, and Joe was staying in the dorms with two of his teammates. We planned to get married once I had completed my junior year. But after my sophomore year, a close friend back home wrote to us that both of our families were in need of help. Our parents never would have asked for help. Joe and I dropped out of college and moved back home. Joe's family farm had declined so much in the short time we were gone. We were married at the courthouse in Havenridge and tried to divide our time, keeping both places going.

"My parents passed within two months of each other. After some time, Joe's mother died, and I moved into his father's house with Joe. I tried to maintain the two houses. Joe cared for both farms, but it was overwhelming. His father was a proud man, with his wife gone and having to rely on his son, it caused him to go into a deep depression. His health spiraled down and three months later, Joe had to arrange his father's funeral. After that, we moved back here. We decided to keep this place and sell Joe's family farm. Mr. and Mrs. Wilson's farm was far too big for Joe to keep up by himself. His dad wouldn't have anything to do with selling the place when he was alive. That's the way it is around here, you don't sell family homes. Places are passed down from generation to generation. Family roots go deep here."

Betsy shared information about the town. I learned that it underwent a renovation a few years earlier. Things changed for a while. Some of the older residents hated the town renovation and decided to sell their farms. A few who owned acres of vacant land either sold the land or built newer, more modern homes, then sold both land and house together. During that time, Sarah moved to Havenridge and bought the general store.

"For the most part, families tended to hold on to older, statelier homes," Betsy said. "After the upheaval of the renovation, things settled down and slowly crept back to the way they were before."

I found out that the residents who wanted to leave had, and that open window of opportunity for new people to move to Havenridge was slammed shut by the end of the renovation. I figured that my hope to move to Havenridge was just a pie in the sky wish, especially considering the stories Betsy told. Then one day, she called me with news about the Brewer house going up for sale. She saw the file at the courthouse releasing the house from probate and knew it would be going on the market.

Betsy said, "Stephanie, to get the chance to buy one of the grand old homes like the Brewer house, you have to have the luck of the Irish working for you."

Whether you want to call it luck or destiny, that's how I learned about the house before anyone in town did and how I was able to buy it.

There had been some out-of-town investors who had inquired about the house. However, they lost interest after the first year. Legal red tape stalled things and the house sat empty for more than two years.

The Brewer house had a rich history. I immediately set an appointment to see it and Betsy filled me in with its history. The Brewers had been the oldest living family in Havenridge up until Mabel Brewer died. The courthouse records dated the family back as far as the early sixteen hundreds. Miss Brewer, which is how she was known, passed away at the age of ninety-eight. She never married, never had any children.

Also, I learned that Johnson Realty was named as executor in Mabel Brewer's will and had been instructed to sell the property. The will designated that profits from the sale would be split among the two schools in town and the public library.

After signing the contract to buy the house, I went to tell Betsy. She beamed and said, "Luck of the Irish, I tell you, Stephanie. You must belong in that house for a reason."

I hoped she would never find out that my reason for moving to Havenridge was not so honorable. The Brewer house would become my hideout.

The Brewer House

The first time I drove out to see the house, Miss Johnson gave me typical country directions. She said, "Follow the road out of town going west until you come to where it splits; the road will curve to the right, then go one mile and it's the big Victorian house right after Roy Parker's old farm." As if everyone would know Roy Parker's farm, even out-of-towners.

I fell in love with the old Victorian instantly. The fact it needed a lot of work seemed just the thing to keep me busy during my sleepless nights.

After seeing the house, I found myself excited about the days ahead. I started thinking about my move, which Steve thought was the worst thing for me to do. I began to think that maybe it was the first right thing that I had done in the last two years.

I remember his shocked expression when I told him I bought a house and would be moving for real. My heart sank when I saw his worry. "Steve, I need to make the move, and I need to do it by myself without any help from you."

Of course, I had to argue long and hard to have my wishes honored. He wanted to drive the truck, but I assured him that it was barely bigger than a van and I could handle it. The only reason I think I won the argument was I played on Steve's sympathy. I explained that I had gone from our parents' home to marriage with Daniel, which never gave me a chance to stand on my own. I wanted to do things by myself and be a grown-up, once and for all. Of course, I didn't share that my new start included lies and secrets about my past to people in the new town. Steve believed strongly that the only way to live was to be truthful and be open with your life. If I can keep this small, but nosy town and my brother from colliding than I won't have to share my past. Thus, I hoped to keep Steve at bay, at least for a while.

Nevertheless, I had won the first round of my battle to make a new life. On Saturday, April 12th, I drove into town in a U-Haul truck, my car in tow, which unbeknownst to me started prying eyes watching me.

Weeks later, I told Betsy that I felt an uneasiness with the people that they seemed to have with me. She explained, "Folks in this town are set in their ways. They have old-time thinking about them. People here have close community ties, good values, and treasure family. They're good folks, but don't change easily. A single woman, moving by herself, let alone driving a truck, can't help but raise a few eyebrows. Give them time."

Not long after moving in, the neighbors came bearing homemade cakes and cookies to welcome me. In time, I'd started to understand Betsy's words about how the people of Havenridge saw outsiders. However polite and neighborly they welcomed me, it didn't mean I was accepted. Their good wishes felt untrue and left me with a feeling of being on the outside of an exclusive society.

I'd been to town at least a dozen times in the first month after moving into my house. I stopped at the country store to pick up food, a hammer, nails, paint, and gardening supplies, to name a few things. There was an endless list of repairs to be done. All rooms had to be painted and I wanted to plant a flower garden. Remnants of what must've been a garden showplace at one time begged for life again. I was developing a type of bond with the former owner, Miss Mabel, and felt a sense of duty to return the beauty to her homestead.

With every trip to the general store, I'd stay and visited with Sarah. I discovered even though most of the people came to town once a week and saw Sarah when they stopped in the general store, they still considered her an outsider or stranger. Then they would go across the street to Kathy's Second-Hand Shop. They didn't mind cashing in on the results of the renovation by selling their unwanted items to Kathy. Items that had been collecting dust in their attics, which visitors traveling through would buy for big bucks.

The neighboring town of Milledgeville brought many travelers to Havenridge. Sarah said everyone was more than happy to receive money from their items even though they thought the whole world had gone crazy paying for old things. Sarah told me that once the town council had approved of all building plans, they immediately started designing a brochure to put in Milledgeville's welcome center to attract travelers.

She showed me the brochure. It had an artist rendering of the quaint town with shops and on the back was a photograph of the beautiful waterfall at the town's edge. Even without a motel, people were stopping in Havenridge on the way to Milledgeville. Every time they would stop and buy something. I guess money makes everything better.

One morning while talking to Sarah, I asked if she needed someone to help at the store. She was always working no matter what time I came into the store. I needed a job to fill my day and I hoped she would welcome some time off. I didn't need to work for the money. I bought Miss Mabel's home for a fraction of the money Daniel paid me for my share of our home. When all the legal matters were settled, I was left financially comfortable.

"Sarah, I was wondering if you could use some help in the store."

Despite what I had thought, being alone in that big house, no matter how much painting and work I did, I needed to connect with someone.

"I would like to get a part-time job and . . . well; you seem to be working every time I come in. Could you use a salesperson?"

"Betsy comes in a couple of days a week to help." She paused as if thinking. "It does seem to be getting busier lately." Sarah looked at me in a questioning manner. "I thought you were busy fixing up your house."

"I am. There's still a lot to do." I liked Sarah, I felt I could talk to her and maybe we could become friends. "I'm not going to be finished with restoring the house for months. I need to have something to keep me from going stir crazy besides painting and coming in to buy more supplies."

It was true. Although everyone in the town was friendly, it was still apparent they considered me "That single woman who had no business living alone in that big house." Those were the exact words I had overheard one day while shopping. However, my self-induced exile couldn't go on forever. I needed to make friends and Sarah seemed a perfect candidate.

Now I understood why Betsy seemed to love our chats. She knew everybody but somehow didn't seem to fit in, either. Maybe the reason I wanted to work for Sarah had been the same reason Betsy worked in the store, too. Betsy aired a loneliness that I just couldn't put my finger on even though it was obvious that she and Joe were totally in love with each other.

"Okay, I guess I could use another hand," Sarah said. "I would love it if you worked in the mornings on the days Betsy doesn't come in." No sooner than the words left her mouth, she said, "No maybe you could work afternoons."

She barely had spoken again and she changed, again. "No. Oh, I don't know." She waved her hand dismissing herself. "Whatever you want to work, but if you could work mornings, that's what I'd like."

She babbled on about Betsy coming in the mornings and it allowed her to be at home to eat breakfast with her girls. I recognized the signs. Betsy wasn't the only one lonely. I knew from experience that being married could be a lonely life. Married, but still being lonely, can make some people overwork or even obsess at trying to please everyone. Not to mention, that many times loneliness can cause some to talk excessively.

It seemed like Sarah's only concern was making me happy, rather than giving me schedule options. But maybe I was wrong. It could just be the way of people in small towns. Betsy's husband, Joe, said often, "Country folks aim to please."

"You could open the store," Sarah continued, rambling on, "and stay until somewhere between two or two-thirty. Then I could eat breakfast with my girls every day and do some errands after I drop them at school. I don't need to check references. I can tell you're a good person. You can start working whenever you want."

No references? That definitely must be a country way.

Orlando was still rather small. It hadn't changed much, even with Disney World recently built near Kissimmee. I figured that it would change soon with all the growth happening around it, but still, it was big enough that businesses there checked references before hiring someone. Country living was going to take time to get used to.

"I feel I've known you all my life," Sarah said. "It'll be fun having you work here. Besides, my husband Tony says I treat the store like a new baby and spend too much time here. But really, I just like being around people. Being a mother is wonderful, but sometimes you want to talk about something other than Big Bird."

Bingo. She's not as happy as she shows to everyone.

* * *

Working at the store gave me just the right amount of personal connection, while still allowing me to keep my secret. Some days before heading home from work, I would stop to visit with Betsy. Soon my life fell into a comfortable routine

I found out on one of my visits at Betsy and Joe's that they were only second generation living in Havenridge. Both Joe and Betsy's grandparents had lived in a big city somewhere in the north. Betsy knew most of the town's history because of growing up here. Nevertheless, neither she nor Joe would ever be truly a Havenridge native. That designation went to families who went back three, four, and five generations. Betsy told me, "Unless your family is third-generation living here, you'll always be considered a newcomer."

I still liked the town and the people, even with their opinion of newbies. There was a comfortable and a serenity feeling, for any generation living, to appreciate. I still believed that Havenridge was the right move for me. Even though I wasn't finished with fixing the house up, it was beginning to reflect my style. I had a job to occupy some of my time and I felt as if I was settling into a comfortable spot. This was where I belonged.

Now if I could just keep Steve from coming to visit me, my past will be safe.

Sarah

Sarah was thirty-four and packed full of energy. I visualized her as a blond-haired Tasmanian Devil character with a smile and a friendly caring nature, always plowing a smoother way for others. The way she had insisted on helping me find a place to stay that first night showed me that she was protective and sensitive. To call a friend—without hesitation—and ask if a total stranger could come over and stay showed that Sarah was a trusting person. That kind of genuine type has a way of influencing the people around them. Maybe that's why I felt I could trust her. Trusting others had disappeared from my life for quite some time. Trust makes you vulnerable. I wasn't sure if I was ready to be that defenseless again.

Despite trying to maintain barriers, it didn't take long for me to become great friends with Sarah. She didn't pry so the friendship worked for me. I think she welcomed the friendship as much as I needed it.

On the other hand, Betsy was different. Although she was as genuine and caring as Sarah, Betsy seemed to delight in sharing idle gossip. It helped fill in all the gaps for me, but I worried that she couldn't keep a secret.

With Sarah, I not only felt safe, but comfortable sharing information with her. Still, I knew to share only the right information.

My working in the mornings at the store gave Sarah time to spend at home. Nevertheless, most days Sarah would come in early after she'd dropped her daughters off at school. A quick stop at home first to make lunch for us, then she'd come into the store, carrying bags of food. Arriving before eleven most days, so we could eat lunch together.

We'd giggle like teenagers, visiting and eating. She had a husband and two beautiful little girls. I knew she shouldn't need to fill her time spending lunch with me. I envied her because she could make the simplest dishes, like her chicken salad, into a gourmet wonder. She made it with almond slices, apples, celery, and seasoned with salt, pepper, and a hint of curry powder. I remember the first time Sarah brought it in and I marveled about how good it tasted.

"I love that you like my chicken salad," she said. "I usually have to eat it plain because my Michelle doesn't like anything crunchy. That's Michelle. She's eight and very mature for her age, except when it comes to food. She's a very picky eater. Unlike Abby, who'll eat anything. Abby's a real tuffy. She may look like the delicate one because she's the fair-haired one, but she's a rough and tumble type."

Sarah paused and took another bite of chicken, putting her napkin in front of her mouth as she chewed, she spoke. "If Abby was the first one I had, I don't know if I'd have been brave enough to have another baby."

She blotted her mouth. "Oh—who am I kidding! I love having kids." Hardly stopping to take a breath and she continued. "If I had my way I'd have a half dozen, but Tony, he . . . . well, it's different with him. He *does* love the girls, but he likes to be first. He likes the freedom that not having children gives you."

She seemed so delighted talking endlessly about her daughters, it was a wonder she finished her lunch that day.

As Sarah chattered away, my mind wandered back to the day I met her girls. It was a Friday and they were off school for a teacher's holiday. It's strange that they call it that because the teachers are the only ones who have to go to school on teacher holidays and work.

***

I was working in the store with Sarah. The front door flew open and in ran the most precious little girls calling Mommy, Mommy. Sarah came around the counter.

"Girls, here I am. Quiet down, use your inside voices."

Sarah turned to me and apologized, explaining that they think of the store as an extension of their home. She introduced Michelle and Abby and they both politely said, "How do you do."

"Well, I'm just fine," I answered. "How are you? Are you enjoying your day off from school?"

After listening to what they had done in the morning, they explained they were grown up enough to walk to the store all by themselves. They said their father was getting a haircut at the barbershop.

Sarah certainly knew her daughters. They were as different as night and day.

Michelle was more reserved and reminded me of the nursery rhyme, "Sugar and spice and everything nice."

Abby was full of life, talked a mile a minute, and asked questions about everything.

"Where do you live? You know my Mommy owns this store. I guess that makes her your boss. You're pretty. Are you a mommy, too?" Never waiting for any answers.

Both girls were so sweet. They came in often after that day. It surprised me that I didn't get depressed with thoughts of Lily when they were around. I felt a happiness that I didn't think was possible to feel anymore.

***

"Hellooo?" Sarah said as she pointed to the bowl of chicken salad. "Pass the chicken salad. Boy, you were zoned out."

"Sorry," I said as I passed the bowl. As Sarah dipped out another spoonful from the Tupperware container, she asked, "Stephanie, have you ever been married?"

I tried not to look startled and answer nonchalantly, "Yes, but we were very young. I married my high school sweetheart."

"Tony and I met in our first year of college," Sarah said. "The next year we got married. Six months later, I was pregnant with Michelle. I dropped my classes because I had morning sickness and never went back. But Tony finished with honors."

"I met Daniel and I got married right after my high school graduation," I said. "I never went to college."

"Wow. What, happened to break you two up?" Then Sarah's eyes widened and her face reddened. "Oh, Stephanie, I'm sorry. I shouldn't have asked."

"No, it's all right," I replied, trying again to act casual. "Well, I think when you marry that young, you don't know who you are, yet. Sometimes you grow into someone you don't recognize, a different person. And sometimes that person doesn't fit with the one you're married to anymore. Anyway, he's in my past."

"Yeah, I know what you mean, Stephanie. Years can change everything. I think that when you get married, you can lose pieces of yourself and become someone else." Sarah's voice had a distant sound as if she was more speaking to herself.

Tony and Sarah seemed to be in sync with each other as parents, but not as much as a couple. I saw a little bit of Tony in both girls: intelligent, friendly, and genuinely nice. Sarah said he made his living as an architect, which is how they ended up in Havenridge. He worked on the town's renovation. After his company finished the project, they decided to take a leap-of-faith into a new life and moved to Havenridge.

I remember Sarah's words. "We knew it would be a perfect town for raising a family. Tony started his drafting business. He always had wanted his own business."

She explained that with his business connections from working at the large architectural firm, it made the transition to freelance work rather easy. They used the profit from the sale of their home and put a down payment on their house in Havenridge. Tony loved the architecture of the old houses in the area. Sarah cashed in the money from the savings program she had at her work and bought the store.

Sarah exclaimed that Havenridge was all about new starts.

I thought about it. My move was originally about escape. But now it seemed more like a new start, too. I felt like a new person emerging from inside of me. A mixture, one part *original me*, and one part *the me after marrying Daniel*, and the final part the *new me*. Sarah was right about time changing a person.

S.O.S.

Friday was delivery day to the store for new merchandise. Therefore, Sarah's husband planned his workday at home on Fridays to help out. Both Sarah and I could work bell to bell, as it is referred to in retail. Sarah didn't need to worry about picking up the children or having to be at the house with them after school on those days. Tony also stayed home one other day so she had a full day to merchandise, order, do office work, or whatever duties that needed her attention.

Sarah suggested we reserve each Friday for a long lunch together to break up the busy day of unpacking, marking merchandise, and restocking.

One particular Friday, during lunch, I jokingly gave Sarah and myself a nickname. You know the way some people tend to pin nicknames on their friends, like the three musketeers.

It started purely by accident when I said, "Sarah, you've been a lifesaver for me. There is only so much holding up in a house that can be tolerated. Only so much fixing up and painting before a person starts running out of things to do. I needed this job to keep from going stir crazy and save my hands from permanently being calloused. But it has become more than just a job. I've found a new friend in the process."

Sarah giggled and said, "Well, I don't really want to confess this, because you'll probably want a raise, but you've been an unexpected lifesaver for me, too. I didn't know how much I needed a friend in this closed-up community. Don't get me wrong, people here are nice, but they don't really accept *outsiders* like us. I needed a friend, too, other than Betsy. Betsy's great, but you, Stephanie, you feel more like a sister."

"You know what we *outsiders* need? Our own secret club! Let the other people be the outsiders," I said defiantly. In school, I had hated the cliques that kept some people out. Especially the ones who acted so superior over the other students. "What we need is a code or password, that'll be a secret just between us."

Sarah laughed, took a bite of sandwich, and said, "Yeah, that'll teach them. Let them be the outsiders for a change."

Snapping my fingers, I said, "I have it! We'll use our names. My name is Stephanie Oliver, take the first letter of my first and last name and we'll add the letter of your first name. As your daughters say, 'Wha-la!' We'll be the S.O.S. Team. Forever saving each other. It'll be our secret—just between you and me."

It was set after that day; we had our club with a secret code. We started bestowing greetings of, "Hello, S.O.S." and "How's your day going, S.O.S.?" When problems cropped up, we'd looked at each other and said, "Sounds like it's time for the S.O.S Team."

Anyone in the store hearing us would look concerned as if we had just escaped the loony bin and would make a quick exit. It was very understandable because we would giggle and act like schoolgirls. I guess this gave added fuel to the town's endless gossiping about the strange outsiders. But we didn't care. It was great fun.

It became a silly way to reverse the tables, making Sarah and I the members of an exclusive club. After all, we were from the generation that grew up during Woodstock. This was just a new way to fight the older establishment. When we were younger, we had songs with our hidden language that had secret meanings, like "Snow Pilot," "Magic Carpet Ride," not to mention the lyrics of the Doors, "you can't get much higher." So, we indulged ourselves in our childish secret code, which bonded our friendship.

Maybe the person I used to be, my younger and more carefree self, wasn't lost completely. As life stomps on you, you don't recognize how much of your true personality gets eroded, unless something happens to take you out of that altered world. If it hadn't been for Havenridge and Sarah, I might never have realized the extent of my erosion. And if Daniel hadn't left me, the true Stephanie could have been lost forever. I was starting to feel strong, like in the past, with each day passing.

Sarah snapped the lid on the container of chicken salad. "We need to get back to work or we'll never get all the stock unpacked and put on the shelves."

"Okay," I answered. I thought about the secrets I had moved with me and one of the boxes back at my house. *I don't need any reminders of my past. Perhaps now is the time to get rid of those newspapers that I brought. Besides, I wouldn't want anyone to find them.*

Packing Up Memories

ORLANDO, MONTHS EARLIER.

When Steve saw me boxing up the newspapers with my other things for the move to Havenridge, his face saddened. "Steph, why are you taking those papers with you? It's over," he said. "You need to forget about it. Let it go!"

Somehow throwing them away was like throwing away part of Lily. I tried to explain it to Steve.

"They have dates; it's like a kind of family history."

"No, it's not! They only hold lies," he argued, "and a record of a witch-hunt. You were always a good mother. Not the person the newspapers wrote about."

"That's not what the district attorney thought. Probably still thinks." I sealed the box, picked it up, and walked out of the room. Under my breath, I mumbled, "Not having evidence to prove in court isn't the same as being innocent."

***

PRESENT DAY-MILLEDGEVILLE

It was my day off. I had planned a full day of organizing pantries and going through my clothes closet, ditching all the things I hadn't worn since moving from Orlando.

My mind kept going back to the box of newspapers that Steve and I argued about before I left. It had taken a lot of time but I was now realizing that he had been right. It was crazy to keep them. Why should I store them in the living room closet? If I was starting fresh, why not destroy them? Dredging through the articles was the last thing that I needed today. I thought about the district attorney in Orlando and figured if he wanted to rekindle an investigation he would've already done it by now. Saving newspapers filled with hatred was pointless. Keeping that box to haunt me in the house was insane. Besides, each headline would forever be burned into my mind. I didn't need the evidence of my past around when I wanted to start over. Still, one particular headline would always haunt me and I knew I would never forget it. It was the one that cost me the last friends I had in my life: *Mother Questioned in Death of Daughter.*

I looked over to the clothes on the bed. *That's enough clothes to throw away. If I clean any more out of my closet, I'll have to become a nudist.* I had to face it; the time had come to get rid of those newspapers. I marched downstairs and crossed the living room.

The wood floors that I painstakingly refinished were beautiful. The large living room and the wood floors were two of the things that had attracted me to the Brewer home in the first place. When I originally came with the real estate agent to see the house, she focused only on the big lawn and lush gardens that used to be there. I had to ask four times to see the inside of the house. Once inside, she ignored the deteriorating condition and the old, dull floors that needed attention. She swung open the closet door in the living room and said, "Of course, houses built in the year that this one was, all have the most wonderful closets." She pivoted around to face me and added, "But I'm sure you will spend most of your time in the garden."

Thinking back, I think she had been trying to *will* me blind to all the repairs the house needed. She must have thought if a single woman noticed the old damaged floors that it would destroy any hope of selling the house.

The prospect of hours buried in hard work had been just what I had wanted and needed. Nevertheless, Miss Diane Johnson, of Johnson Realty, had been quite a character. She didn't even seem to notice I had fallen in love with the old Victorian. Later, I found out from Betsy that Diane's family owned the realty office for over twenty years. Everyone including Diane assumed she would go into a real estate career after graduating from high school, which she did. However, from what I had experienced about her sales ability, she had chosen the wrong career. She kept on talking and trying to sell me the house, instead of closing the sale by asking me what I thought. Finally, I got through to her that the two things missing to finalize the sale were a contract and a pen for my signature.

Enough stalling and reminiscing about when I first saw the house. The box of newspapers was beckoning me from the "most wonderful," as the realtor had pointed, living room closet. I had pushed the box with the newspapers inside to hide them away.

Swinging the door open with the same zest as Diane Johnson had on that first day and I stepped inside. The closet was huge, almost the size of a small bathroom, with shelves on both sides. A rod extended at the end from side-to-side for sweaters and winter coats to hang.

I crouched down, leaning forward on my knees, and pulled two boxes of photo albums out of my way. Reaching back for the third box, which was hidden in the darkness, I had to stop because of a long trench coat dangled in my face. I pushed it away and felt the box with the newspapers in it. As I fingered along the edge of the box to grab it, something scraped my knuckles.

"Ouch!" I pulled my hand back. Whatever it was had pierced my skin, leaving three droplets of blood-forming on my fingers.

I hadn't noticed any protruding nails or splinters of wood on the walls of the closet when I had refinished the floor in there. Nevertheless, something on the back wall had caught my hand. I pulled the box gingerly out of the closet, making sure not to cut myself again, and dragged it into the living room. I took a seat on the couch, rubbing my injured hand. The horrid box on the floor at my feet goaded me. It would be easy to start a repair in the closet, instead of facing my real task at hand. Ignoring the all too easy diversion of whatever caught my skin in the closet; I slit open the box with a razor and unfolded the sides back. I wanted to make sure I had the correct box.

It was the right box, inside were the stacks of newspapers. On the very top, staring up at me was an Orlando Sentinel paper with a sickening headline:

Mother Administered the Fatal Dose of Medicine to Daughter.

The familiar wave of nausea crashed over me. My hands shook as I fingered through the rest of the papers. A cold sweat crept over my body. My skin was clammy like that of a corpse, the only difference was I still walked and talked. Each paper held endless streams of accusations.

Steve had been right. The box and its contents had to go. But, how? If I burned the contents, I might draw attention from whoever lived in the house up on the hill.

My head whirled. Time, I needed time to think this through before doing anything. As I unconsciously massaged the scratch on my hand, my thoughts returned to the closet.

If I found that nail, removed it, and patched the hole. . . . that would give me time to figure out how to dispose of the papers.

I went to the closet. I needed to clear away the hanging clothes so I would be able to see and work. Grabbing an armload of coats and jackets, I turned and looked for a place to put them.

Of course, the couch! I threw them down on the cushions next to the open box and returned to the closet. Unfortunately, the depth of the now empty closet created a dark, cavernous opening. I needed a flashlight to see and remembered that I put one in the catch-all drawer in the kitchen for safekeeping last week after stumbling around the house when the power went out during a thunderstorm. I had sworn I wouldn't be caught in the dark like that again.

With the flashlight in hand, I entered the closet on hands and knees, searching the interior wall, looking for the culprit of my injury. The closet walls were smooth cedar planks. No splinters, nothing to cut a finger. Then, I noticed that the wood on the back wall had a different color in a small area. There, several of the planks seemed uneven, and one, in particular, seemed to stick out ever so slightly from the remaining planks. I moved in closer to inspect it and saw that the protruding wood had two small hinges down low near the baseboard.

Too low for a door, unless I was Alice in Wonderland, I thought. Moving the light over to the opposite side revealed a flat piece of metal bent into a hook shape, which rested inside an eyelet blackened with age. Lower my face down to see better and rubbed my fingers across the hook and eyelet.

"Ouch." The metal was jagged. I had found what scratched my finger—twice, now. There, near the base of the closet's back wall was a two-foot by two-foot door cut into the cedar planks.

Strange place for a door, even in an old Victorian house in the countryside of Georgia. And even odder, why would one of the Brewers cut and build a door there? The only possible answer was that whatever lies beyond the door, someone thought it was so terrible that it needed to be kept from the rest of the world. I tried to unlatch the hook, but it was rusted stuck. Remembering that I had left tools upstairs while fixing a leak under the bathroom sink a few days ago, I raced to get them.

Pliers might work. I could use a screwdriver to wedge and force the door open if the wood was warped.

Upstairs, I gathered an assortment of tools, including a hammer. Then back to the kitchen's catch-all drawer for some WD-40. That stuff could work miracles to loosen things when bare muscle wouldn't work.

I entered the closet armed with a plan of attack. No telling how long the secret space had been closed off. The house was built over 100 years ago. The Brewer family had been the only owners. Miss Mabel had been 98 when she died. I wondered if she knew about the space. It wasn't likely that she would cut into the wood wall of the closet herself. It was my guess she didn't know about it. Besides, why would an old-maid schoolteacher need a hidden space in her living room closet?

I oiled the hinges and the hooked lock then wedged the screwdriver in and pushed up. The hook gave away, and I was able to push it out of the eyelet. Then I wedged the screwdriver into the seam of the door and tried to pry it open.

It didn't budge.

Good thing I thought to get the hammer. Placing the flashlight under my arm and adjusting it to point the beam of light at the door. I started pounding the screwdriver.

It wasn't working so I wiggled the screwdriver, putting as much force as I could into hammering and pushing. One last shove and . . . I plummeted down, smashing my shoulder against the wall when it gave way and the door flung open. The flashlight spun out from under my arm, spinning beams of light around like a disco dance mirror ball.

As I rubbed my shoulder, I leaned forward and peered into the opening. I couldn't determine the size or depth of the hiding place because it was a sea of black. A musty smell assaulted my nose. That same odor penetrated many of the older homes in these parts. Residents around here had a habit of keeping everything. From string rolled into balls (you never know when you might have to tie something up) to their great-great grandmother's wedding gown. The practice of this never-ending hoarding generated the aged scent along with the smell of mothballs.

I had forgotten how gagging and nauseating the odor was because up until now, I thought I had managed to clean away all the remains of it in the house. Coughing and rubbing my watering eyes, I felt around for the flashlight. My fingertips touched pieces of the flashlight that apparently had unscrewed apart. Fumbling around, I found the batteries and the rest of the parts and reassembled the flashlight and pushed the switch—it worked. I tried to focus the beam into the black hole. Inside were books, or papers, and a box. I pulled them out onto the floor.

Off in this distance, as I thumbed through what I had discovered, I realized a there had been a constant, irritating noise. I listened and heard it again. The noise was someone knocking at my front door, and it had been going on for some time.

Then the knocking stopped, followed by the creak of my front door.

A voice called from inside the house! "Hello, Is anyone home?"

I jumped up, banging my head on the coat rod. "Ouch!"

The crazy thought ran through my mind that this must be the day for getting beat up by my house.

"Just a minute," I called out. *What is it with country people walking in uninvited?*

Hurrying out. Closing the closet door behind me, I muttered. "If I wanted you to come into my house, I would've answered the door."

"Oh, I'm sorry. I heard you hammering and thought that you didn't hear my knock."

I stopped dead in my tracks to see a pretty girl with blonde hair pulled into a ponytail standing behind the back of my couch. "Around here, people expect you to let yourself in if they don't come to the door." She was holding a plate of cookies. "I didn't mean to be rude."

At least, I had time enough to stop her from seeing what I had uncovered in the closet. Whatever it was I had found.

Her eyes scanned the couch with the clothes. "I figured that enough time had passed that I needed to extend my welcome to you."

Her eyes swept the couch again and beyond toward the open box of newspapers. I rushed forward, grabbing an armful of clothes off the couch and threw them on top of the box. "It's quite all right. I was just . . . uh, cleaning the coat closet. Please take a seat."

I didn't think she had time to read that wretched headline. Besides, my name was further down in the article. I wanted to keep the secrets of the contents of the closet, and my secrets contained. Especially from a blond, pony-tailed girl, I didn't even know.

She introduced herself as Leanne Thompson and said she had moved here about a year ago. I guessed she was around my age, maybe a couple of years younger. It's hard to judge because she said she was single with no children. I'm terrible at judging ages. I usually ask about children, everyone loves talking about their children, once I know their children's ages I can estimate the age of the person. Most people marry around age nineteen or twenty. Add a year or two before having the first baby, then add the age of the oldest child, and you have a pretty good idea how old they are, but with no children to use as a gauge I don't have a clue.

The freckles across a turned-up nose gave her a youthful appearance. Her ponytail seemed to bob and swing as she talked. "I have a confession to make. I had the cookies sitting on the counter to bring by but it's not why I came today." She looked distraught and her eyes began to tear up. "I don't lie well, but I didn't want to just come over here and blurt it out."

"Oookay. What are you trying to say?"

"Betsy Wilcox just called me from Sarah's store. She didn't have your number, so she called me since I'm just up the road, on the hill," she stammered. "She didn't know what else to do, Betsy, that is."

She started to cry.

Good grief, I lose my temper once and I have a sweet, innocent young girl crying.

I didn't want to be mean, but I wanted her out of my house. My mind was on the contents of the closet. "Just tell me what's wrong."

"Well, Betsy told me Sarah left her to watch the store for a few hours. While Betsy was cleaning off some shelves, she knocked over a lit candle displayed above a stack of kitchen towels. They caught on fire. You know how upset Betsy can get," Leanne said. "She tried to put out the fire and I guess it got away from her. She had to call the fire department. I suppose there's a bit of damage."

Poor Leanne looked unnerved, too, but continued explaining. "Betsy was crying so hard." By now, Leanne had composed herself and blotted her eyes. "Betsy said she wasn't able to get ahold of Sarah and was too frightened to call Tony. I could hardly understand her. I felt so bad for her. I promised I'd come over and get you. All she kept saying was that you would know what to do."

"All right, I'll go to the store and see what's going on. Do you want to ride with me?" I asked.

"I can't, I left soup cooking on the stove."

I got my purse, retrieved a paper with a list of things I needed from the store, and turned it over to jot my phone number down. I went to give it to Leanne but now she seemed to be thinking about going with me.

She was talking to herself. "If I go home and turn the soup off . . . I better turn on some lights, in case I don't get back until dark. Oh, if I'm that long, I better put the soup in the fridge, but it'll be too hot—"

"Leanne," I interrupted. "No sense making plans to go. Go home, I'll go and find out what happened. I'll call you if we need you."

"You don't think you'll need my help? I could take care of things at home and then drive into town to the store."

"No, let me check it out first," I said.

55

Today was Sarah's day to work. I wondered what was so important that it took her away from the store. And why did she call Betsy and not me?

I would get some answers soon enough, the store was only a ten-minute drive. When Leanne and I walked outside, we could hear sirens in the distance.

I paused and locked the front door to ensure that nobody else could wander in while I was gone, securing, for now, all the secrets inside my house. Whatever one of the Brewers had hidden would remain concealed for a little longer.

Charred Embers and Burning Lies

During the short drive to the store, my mind raced with a million questions. I knew Sarah used to have Betsy come in two days a week. However, once I started working, Betsy asked if she could only come in during the holiday season. So why would Sarah call Betsy instead of me? She might have thought I would be in the middle of a project and wouldn't be able to stop. If one of Sarah's girls had gotten hurt at school, she wouldn't want to wait for me, and Betsy could come immediately. Sarah wouldn't even have to wait for her since Betsy still had a store key.

Something else troubled me. Leanne said that Betsy said on the phone that Sarah left strict instructions not to call Tony for any reason while she was away, "not even if the store was burning down." Why would Sarah forbid Betsy from calling Tony in case of an emergency?

No wonder poor Betsy was so panic-stricken.

Another thing was that Sarah had activated an old mobile phone that she had previously owned once her first daughter was born. Even after Tony started working at home, she kept the mobile phone so the school could reach her anytime she was away from the store. Like on days when she traveled to Milledgeville for new merchandise. It never left her side. Sarah even carried it with her on daily bank runs when making the store deposit. Surely, Betsy had tried calling that number.

Why would Sarah not answer her phone?

So many questions buzzed in my mind. Although mobile phones were getting common in bustling cities, no one owned one in this sleepy little town except for Sarah. That made her reachable at any time, so why wasn't she available now? The whole series of events didn't match up.

***

My mind wandered as I drove to the store, remembering one time when we were working together.

I had been working with Sarah at the store when her phone rang. It was Michelle calling just to say hello. I heard an elderly shopper's comment, "Sarah is just putting on airs, having a mobile phone like some big city executive."

The women shopping with the *old busybody* nodded in agreement and rolled her eyes.

Sarah pretended not to hear them. After ending the call, she said loudly that the modern luxuries made it easy for her girls to have their mother's attention anywhere and anytime. It helped her to be the best mother possible.

***

So now, when there was a real emergency, what could be keeping technology from reaching her?

I pulled into the back parking lot of the store, next to the only fire truck the city of Havenridge owned. A crowd of people was stirring about. Even the men working the farms had left tractors and fields to follow the sounds of the sirens into town. Everyone was there, everyone but Sarah.

Betsy stood on the sidewalk nearly in tears, but in control. I walked toward her and when she saw me, she broke down in crying. "I'm so sorry. I tried to put it out," she explained. "But I'm afraid it got away from me. I had to call for help. I couldn't get Sarah on her phone."

Betsy looked past me with a look of shock. "Oh, no. Here comes Tony."

She leaned in close, grabbing my arm and pulling me toward her. "Please don't tell Tony that I tried to call Sarah. Don't let on that you know anything. And don't tell him that I had Leanne come get you. Make up something about why you're here if he asks you."

Don't let on that I knew anything? The problem was that I didn't know anything and now I was supposed to make up a story of why I was here, and *lie* to Tony.

Betsy wiped away her tears. She watched Tony cross the street. He was heading straight toward us.

"Betsy, what am I supposed to say? He knows it's my day off. He's going to want to know why you're here and not Sarah."

"He knows about me working so he won't ask," Betsy said. "I'll say that Sarah drove out to check on old Mrs. Jenkins because she's been sick. She lives about fifteen miles away. You just need to back up anything I say. He mustn't know we can't get Sarah on the phone."

I frowned, not understanding the reason for all the deception. Apparently, I wasn't the only one with secrets.

"Please Stephanie, I can't tell you why, just don't tell Tony."

The very next second Tony was in front of us. "Good grief, what happened here, Betsy?"

I had never seen Betsy so upset. Even though it felt wrong, I pretended I had just gotten there and knew nothing. I felt I was as much a friend of Tony's as Sarah's, and hated lying to him.

***

SEVERAL MONTH EARLIER:

Tony had been the first person I met in town, after Sarah and Betsy. I had stopped into the store after my house closing and mentioned I had bought the Brewer house. Sarah asked when I'd be back to move in and she insisted that she and her husband would help me. I barely knew her at the time and I had never even seen Tony.

When moving day came, I pulled into my gravel driveway and saw Sarah and Tony sitting on the veranda of the house waiting. Tony worked all day unloading my furniture and even stayed to arrange each piece where I wanted them in all of the rooms. They were both there for hours. The next day when I went into the store to buy some essentials, I noticed a calendar on the wall with my moving day circled with a note "family picnic" crossed through. They had canceled it to help me.

***

Now, I was about to deceive Tony with lies and I didn't even know why.

"There was a small fire," Betsy answered Tony.

"Is everyone all right?" he asked.

"Yes," Betsy said. "A candle fell over and caught some towels on fire."

Tony looked around at the crowd. "Where's Sarah?"

"Sarah's on her way," I said. "Betsy's got everything under control."

Tony seemed satisfied and said he needed to get back to the house. The girls had just come home from school when he heard the sirens. A neighbor was staying with them. Before he left, he asked us to have Sarah call him when she returned, but he never asked where she had gone to.

Once Tony left, I turned to Betsy. "What's going on? Where's Sarah?"

"Stephanie, I can't tell you. It's not up to me to say. You need to accept that and let it be. I left a message on her phone. Anyway, she always checks in by three or four o'clock."

"Always checks in? What do you mean?" I was confused and a bit angry. "You mean she goes off like this a lot?"

I thought Sarah and I told each other everything. After all, we were the S.O.S. pair. At least, I thought there were no secrets between us. I knew I had secrets, but they were necessary. I didn't know who I was angrier with, Sarah for her secrets, or Betsy for not telling them to me. And I thought Betsy liked to gossip. Guess I was wrong about both of them.

I pressed Betsy one more time. She was very sympathetic. However, she firmly stated she couldn't break a confidence. That day I saw a new side of Betsy Wilcox, the side that respected a person's privacy. She genuinely cared deeply about people. Betsy had brought me into a circle of trust when dealing with Tony, while still keeping her promise to Sarah. I felt a bond forming with Betsy. The way I saw it, Sarah had betrayed our friendship with the secret she kept, whatever that was. I wondered how much I did I knew about my S.O.S friend.

The firemen were packing their equipment when the fire chief approached us. He asked me if I could sign his On the

61

Scene form. A full report would be several pages long explaining the details of their call, and a copy of it would be mailed to the store owner in a few days.

Once the truck pulled away, Betsy and I went into the store, to sum up the damages. The place was a mess. Betsy said she was glad I had been there for support when Tony arrived. She was calm and seemed more worried about not talking about Sarah's secret than about the fire.

Up until then, I had comfortably settled into my friendship with Sarah. I'd always felt guilty about not confiding to her about my past, but now I thought, it might have been a good decision to keep my secrets from her. Especially since Sarah hadn't been completely honest with me.

I stood before the wreckage left by the fire. Clearly, Betsy had integrity. The way I saw it, Sarah lied to me by the omission of the truth. I didn't know if there were other lies. Sadly, the S.O.S. pair has no honor. It was just a childish game. Through this accidental event, everything had changed.

I watched Betsy, a new deepening respect for her was developing. She systemically gathered things and efficiently surveyed what could be salvaged. Betsy Wilcox reflected a confident, business-like woman. In all the times I had visited Betsy, I realized that I had never asked anything about her and her life. I had always seen her as a lonely gossip with no history of her own. Looking back, I realized that whenever Betsy spoke about someone, she interjected reasons for their shortcomings or faults. She understood and always showed compassion for them and was never judgmental.

How could I have seen Betsy as so one-dimensional? I felt sincerely sorry I never asked about her personal life. Regret filled me that I had never taken the time to get to know her better.

She helped whenever she was called upon, and when with me, she never asked any questions. I hoped I could start over with Betsy. Maybe we could be friends, not just acquaintances. Betsy definitely was trustworthy.

"Betsy, how long has Sarah been gone?" I asked.

"About three hours," she said as she checked her watch. "She'll be calling in soon."

I bent down and picked through the charred and wet remnants.

"Stephanie, let's not go into this again. I'm not at liberty to discuss where she is," Betsy said. "She's never gone past four-thirty. When and if she wants to tell you, she will. Until that time, you need to respect her privacy."

She threw a handful of blackened towels into a nearby trash can.

"Everyone at some time needs isolation without questions," Betsy continued as she turned around to face me. "I'm really not one to judge, I can understand. I remember once I . . ." She stopped and shook her head as if to erase an unpleasant memory.

"Sarah is a good person," Betsy continued. "Most people have good intentions. They *intend* to do the right thing, but things get in the way. No one can understand the emotions that someone else goes through, not unless you've experienced them first-hand. Nobody should judge others. None of us are free of guilt."

Betsy looked around and then picked up the only clean towel left on the counter. She smelled it, wrinkled her nose, and threw it back down.

She turned to me with her hands on her hips and said, "Sarah will know I called you because you signed the fire report.

So, if you want to stay and help me clean up, I suppose it won't hurt. I would like to get most of this mess cleared away before she gets back. You don't have to stay if you don't want to, Stephanie. I can tell her what happened and fill her in on what Tony knows."

"No, Betsy, I want to stay. You don't have to worry. I won't question her. Tell her that I didn't even ask where she was and that way if she wants to make something up to tell me, she can."

I was more worried about Betsy's feelings than about Sarah. With the events of today, and our commitment not to probe into Sarah's whereabouts; Betsy and I were forming a private bond of friendship. I didn't know how strong it would become, or if it would be long-lasting, but what I did know was beneath the surface, Betsy possessed an inner strength that I admired.

Twenty minutes later, Sarah came charging into the store. "I got your message and came as quickly as I could. Are you all right? You sounded so scared. Did Tony . . . did you call Tony?"

"Tony was here," Betsy said with a strong voice.

"What did you tell him?"

"Slow down," Betsy said gently, looking directly at Sarah. Then she glanced over in my direction to clue in Sarah of my presence. "Everything is under control. Tony heard the sirens and came into town to see what was going on. After I called the fire department, I called Stephanie and she came to help. She signed the fire report. I told Stephanie about your possibly stopping to see old Mrs. Jenkins because she's been ill. Stephanie spoke to Tony and said you'd be back soon." Betsy put her arm around Sarah's shoulder and walked her over to a stool. "We were just going over the damages."

Sarah sat and looked around. Water puddles were on the floor and counters. The things that weren't burned were drenched and soiled from the firefighters' effort to contain the fire. The merchandise left didn't look in any better condition than the fire-damaged items.

"Did you get your errands done?" Betsy prompted Sarah.

"Yes, uh, old Mrs. Jenkins is doing better." Sarah looked dazed and was obviously shaken. "How, the fire ... how did it start?" Then turning to me, not waiting for an answer to her question, she said, "Stephanie, thank you for coming."

Betsy filled Sarah in on the details of the fire. Afterward, Sarah called Tony and then the three of us cleaned up what we could. Sarah decided that she would keep the store closed the next day to finish getting everything back in order. Besides, that would allow her to make the necessary calls to the insurance company uninterrupted by customers.

It was close to ten o'clock when we locked up. Sarah thanked Betsy and said she didn't have to come in the next day, stating that the two of us could handle what was left. I couldn't wait to get home and get into bed. I figured that I wouldn't have any trouble sleeping tonight. I was exhausted.

At home, as I put the key into the front door lock, I remembered the secrets that my living room closet held. It would have to wait. I made my way upstairs to my bedroom as my head swam with so many unanswered questions. I came to this town hoping to make my life simple and to avoid questions from snooping neighbors. However, maybe this town harbored more than just a small-town closeness. Somewhere behind the picturesque setting, it had buried secrets, too.

I collapsed onto my bed, too tired to even change out of my soiled clothes.

I had moved miles away to escape from people who relished in lies and gossiping to seek a simple haven from my past.

Perhaps Havenridge was no different from any other place. Different only in size.

People play games of hide-and-seek with their lives, concealing things from one another. Nothing changes. The only difference between now and then is there are new players.

Remembering Daniel

The buzz of the alarm clock woke me. Having an annoying buzzing waking me from sleep has become the only regular thing in my life. Because of my insomnia, my sleep pattern consisted of me waking up five or six times a night. I never fall back to sleep for good until it's almost time to get up again. This is a pattern that causes me to be so exhausted that I either sleep through the alarm or snooze it until I'm late. My life has become a state of constant contradictions.

I hit the button on the clock and opened my eyes.

I don't even remember closing my eyes.

It was crazy that the best night's sleep I had experienced in years would come after finding out my S.O.S. friend has been less than honest with me. I had found that my secrets were not the only ones in town.

Hope it doesn't take another fire for me to sleep like that again.

Back in Orlando, before everything had happened, I would be up by five-forty a.m. at the latest and be well-rested. I had to rise early to have enough time to get Lily up and dressed. We would talk or she would finish her homework while I cooked a hot breakfast for her. After she ate, I would drive her to school. I never overslept back then.

My life in Havenridge was different. I was different. It was just ten minutes from my front door into town, yet it seemed that I never got to the store on time. I was in a constant state of *lateness*.

I quickly changed out of my wrinkled slept-in clothes and rushed downstairs. Today, I would get to the store on time for once. I locked the front door and started toward the car. The day seemed like any other day, sunny with fluffy, white cotton-ball clouds in a clear blue sky. A mockingbird's song chirped happily in the distance. Even though the day was beautiful and cheerful, Sarah's disappearing act gnawed at me. I didn't know why I was surprised. After everything that had happened in my life, I knew that things can change, and *do* change without any warning.

Why is it so hard for me to accept the fact that in life you cannot depend on anyone or anything? Not Sarah, and not our friendship. Nothing is constant.

I climbed into the car, determined to face the day head-on. After turning the key, I reached over and turned on the radio. I had it set to a channel that played oldies from the 60s and 70s. "Kind of a Drag" by the Buckinghams was playing. A memory flashed in my mind of a summer day during my high school years.

***

It had been a hot summer, with the Fourth of July falling on a Thursday that year. My memory of that day was vivid because I had hoped my parents would let me go to Daytona Beach for the holiday with my five girlfriends; Terri, Joyce, Laura, Patsy, and Barbara. Some of the fathers were planning to take Friday off so they could spend a long weekend with their families. We all were worried about getting permission.

It had been a quiet day. I was in my room looking through some movie magazines. They had pictures of Troy Donahue, Frankie Avalon, and Paul Anka. Then the doorbell rang and I went to answer it. Upon opening it, I saw Terri standing there. Ever since she had gotten her regular driver's license, she'd volunteer to run errands for her mom. Any excuse to take the car out.

Terri started talking immediately. "Hi, Stephanie. I told my mom I'd go get bread at the store, but I don't have to be home with it until dinnertime at five o'clock."

She walked in past me and headed to my bedroom without missing a beat. "Do you want to ride with me?"

I followed her back to my room and we flopped on the bed. "Go to the store for bread?" I rolled my eyes and picked up a magazine. I flipped a page and said, "Oh boy, that'll be great fun."

"We can drive by the Olivers' house on the way. They're having a new roof put on and the guys working on it are hunks. With this heat, most of them have their shirts off."

I continued flipping pages as if I wasn't interested. Terri ignored my acting and asked, "Remember Tommy McDonald? He was a senior last year but dropped out before graduating. He's working for the roofing company the Olivers' have hired. You remember, don't you?"

Of course, I did. Every girl in school knew who Tommy was because he was older than all the other boys, which made him way cool. Although, most of the parents didn't think it was cool because they would snicker that Tommy would be drinking age before graduating high school.

"He was a lot older because he had flunked a bunch of times," Terri reminded me. "Anyway, he's really cute and when I drove by they were all taking a break on the front lawn. Maybe we can stop and talk to him."

The details of that day flooded back. They were as fresh as if it had happened yesterday.

"Okay, Terri, I'll go with you," I said, sitting up on my bed. "But you have to agree that we are only going to drive by and not stop."

"Sure," Terri said.

We drove there and Terri's car radio was playing the same song that now played today.

Kind of a drag, when your baby don't love you. Hearing those words made imagining the scene from so long ago so easy.

Terri had always been so predictable and rarely kept her promises, especially when they were made with an instant response to me. So, when she pulled over in the grass in front of the Oliver's house I wasn't surprised. I pretended to be angry that she broke her word.

"Terri, I thought we weren't stopping? You agreed."

Terri turned off the engine and pulled the key out.

"Yeah, sure, Stephanie. You knew we were stopping. Come on." A second later, Terri was out of the car, waving and calling to Tommy who was sitting in the grass with the rest of the crew.

That was the day I met Daniel. He came out of his house with a pitcher of water and paper cups for the workers. Even though he had lived only two streets away, I had never met him because he went to a private school. Not one of those military schools where parents sent their sons when they were out of control, but one that accepted only the highest caliber of students.

I knew who Daniel was, everyone knew about Daniel. The talk started in the neighborhood about him when we were back in elementary school. It was common knowledge the teachers found it difficult to give him assignments that were even remotely challenging to him.

He was doing high school work by the time he turned ten years old. The public school couldn't keep up with him. His IQ was practically off the charts. The people who didn't have children even knew about Daniel because of an article in the newspaper. The headline had read, *Boy Genius Gets Scholarship to Yale.*

Daniel had earned his high school diploma just one month shy of his sixteenth birthday and then started college. Daniel had been one of only five student researchers assigned to work for a major pharmaceutical company while attending classes. Daniel did the research and earned two degrees, all before turning eighteen years old.

* * *

Kind of a drag, when your baby says goodbye
Kind of a drag
The lyrics blasted from my car radio. My vision blurred as tears welled up. Images of Daniel from those years back when we were so young flashed before me. Reminiscing, I had thought that Terri was stupid for being impressed by the muscle-bound roofers instead of Daniel. Sure, Daniel had been slim with not even the smallest muscle showing, but his dark hair and deep navy-blue eyes had made me tingle. To me, he had a suave and mature nature that the other boys didn't possess. He reminded me of James Bond, minus the gorgeous Bond Girls hanging onto him.

Daniel was intelligent and could explain Einstein's theory with confidence. But then, he seemed lost for words and awkward with small talk.

I could see the scene in my mind, Terri chatting away with Tommy, flirting and giggling. When I tried doing the same with Daniel, he acted disinterested and said he had to go, and started back toward the house.

Now I listened to the same song playing and the far-away images were crystal clear of Daniel walking away from me as the roofers drank the water he had brought out. I had stood in disbelief that he was just leaving me standing in the middle of the grass. But then, he stopped midway between the house and me. He turned, walked back to me, and he asked me out!

Kind of a drag

I had fallen madly in love with his adorable shyness that summer day and that was the start of a wonderful romance.

After that summer ended, I started my senior year and Daniel left for Yale. The distance made the attraction stronger. We had spoken on the phone about his career and my finishing high school and our plans to get married.

The rest was history, no more carefree days for either of us. Our journey from then on moved at groundbreaking speed. One year afterward, we were married.

Kind of a drag.

The music that had transported me back in time, now, managed to jerk me forward to the present and my new reality. It's strange how a simple song can stir up memories and haunt you with your past. A tear escaped and was running down my cheek.

Where did that young couple go who were so in love? "How did everything change between us, Daniel?" I asked and the image of that teenage boy remained in my mind.

Girl, I still love you

I still love you

The song paralyzed me, half of me in my car in Havenridge, Georgia, and the other half of me with Daniel in the past.

I'll always love you

Anyway . . . anyway . . . anyway.

"Who would have known that your love for me would turn into loathing and contempt?" My question asked out loud probably would never have an answer. The hard questions never do. "How could young love turn into hatred and change our lives so quickly?"

Music drenched up the past, like opening a dam. Bringing back the good memories, along with the bad memories ones, too.

"Well, folks that was '*Kind of a Drag*' by The Buckinghams," the DJ voice came through the car speakers. "It was the number one hit on the music billboard back in February 1967. Next up we'll play the hits of 1968, right after this commercial break."

Thoughts of that far-away summer whirled in my head, they needed to be pushed back. I had to live in today. Although, living in today felt more like serving out a sentence of punishment. I reached down, turned off the radio, and pulled out of my driveway.

Minutes later, I pulled into the parking lot behind the store and gathered my things. Once I had felt that I had found a new friend, my S.O.S. friend, someone I knew; but now I wondered if I really knew Sarah at all and whether we were ever truly friends.

I made my way to the back door of the store. Jumbled emotions of anger, suspicion, and betrayal ran through me. Images of Sarah were shrouded with lies and cover-ups. They nagged at me as if I were a teenager again and was being kept out of a secret coven.

Was I being childish? Was I a hypocrite? I had my secrets. Nevertheless, I feared things would never be the same for the S.O.S. pair. Coming to the rescue for each other had restrictions controlled by invisible barriers.

I didn't know if I could keep my promise I made to Betsy as I fought back mixed feelings of anger and betrayal.

I turned the doorknob and walked into the store carrying with me *my lie,* and *my secret.*

A Matter of Trust

When I saw Sarah, I decided not to ask her where she had been before the fire. I would keep my promise to Betsy. I felt I owed it to her. She genuinely wanted to protect Sarah's privacy. I of all people knew the importance of privacy.

"Oh, hi. I'm glad you're here," Sarah said with a smile. "I've cleaned up most everything. We just need to do some rearranging and filling in the empty spaces are left from the burnt towels. Boy, Betsy can really mess you up," Sarah said shaking her head.

I stood there dumbfounded, staring at her.

"Oh, Betsy's always there to help when you need her, but I mean, sometimes you wish you hadn't asked."

I don't believe it! She's actually belittling Betsy. How two-faced can she be?

"Betsy can get so rattled," Sarah continued. "Anyone else who had knocked over a candle probably would've stamped the fire out with another towel. It's not like she had to go find something to suffocate the flames. The fire was on top of a stack of towels, for goodness' sake."

Rattled! Betsy can get so rattled? I had to bite my tongue to keep from saying that Betsy was rattled because she had her mind on keeping the secret Sarah wanted her to keep from everyone. If Betsy hadn't had to worry about who she could and couldn't call, she wouldn't have been rattled. Not to mention worrying about what to say to me. I mashed my lips together in an attempt to hold back the words that were trying to escape. Rebuttals and thoughts raced through my mind.

Sarah stopped arranging the items on the shelf. Turning toward me, she held her hand, palm up, as if gesturing for me to agree with her. "Really, there are times," she continued degrading Betsy. "I've watched her and she seems to be in another world."

In another world, I thought. *How about you? How many worlds are you living in, with your little secrets?*

I couldn't believe what I was hearing from Sarah. What a snip. Who's the hypocrite, now? I stood there trying to compose myself as she continued talking. Then I snapped.

The hell with my promise. I opened my mouth to say something and then thought of Betsy. If I lost it and told Sarah off, I'd be hurting Betsy. Maybe Tony and the girls, too.

Take a deep breath . . . now let it out . . . and count one, two, three—

"Stephanie, what's wrong? You're getting red, are you okay?"

"Yes, I'm fine." *One more deep breath.* "It's probably because I rushed to get here. I didn't want to be late."

I forced a smile and started straightening some merchandise on a shelf next to me. Then I turned back to Sarah. "You know, Betsy was wonderful yesterday. You weren't here. She took charge. She did everything right. Nobody was here to help her, you know."

"Oh, I know, she's a dear. I didn't mean anything."

"Yeah, she said something about not being allowed to call Tony? I think that's another reason she might have been rattled."

Here was her chance. If Sarah wanted to let me in her little secrets, I gave her the opportunity. We'll see if she takes it.

"Oh no, she could've called Tony. I told her he was working on a project and that he had a deadline coming up. She must've gotten confused, thinking I didn't want him disturbed. You don't know Betsy that well, Stephanie. She gets things mixed up sometimes."

What a bitch! Trying to make Betsy sound feeble.

Betsy was our age and the sweetest person I've ever met. She was loyal, not a liar like some people. My anger was building like a tidal wave inside of me. I wished that I could tell her that the charade was over, but I had promised Betsy.

"I guess so, you've known her longer," I said curtly. "By the way, how is old Mrs. Jenkins? Has she been ill for very long? Betsy never said." I didn't promise Betsy I wouldn't taunt Sarah.

"What?"

"Old Mrs. Jenkins?" I looked blankly at her, while I inwardly enjoyed seeing Sarah squirm. "Isn't that where you were when the fire started? Didn't you drop by to see her?" I wasn't going to make it easy to keep up her deception.

Seconds passed. Her eyes twitched back and forth, as she thought. Then, a smile grew across her face. Sarah made a chuckling sound while shaking her head. "Betsy, Betsy, Betsy. She *really* was confused. We talked about Mrs. Jenkins because she's been ill, but I had to go to Milledgeville to check on some stuff for the store. That's why she couldn't get me. My mobile phone doesn't work between here and there. Not many towers because there are very few mobile phones in use in this part of the country."

Exasperated, I let out a gasp. *Boy, she must buy her nerve by the truckload.* She couldn't even remember what she said yesterday. I never had suspected her to be a liar, probably because she did it so effortlessly. I'm glad I didn't confide in her about Lily. She can't be trusted.

We worked until one-thirty, and then Sarah asked if I wanted to get some lunch from the diner down the street and bring it back to the store so we could eat together.

No, I didn't want to eat lunch with her. Sarah and I weren't friends. Friends don't lie to each other. I should've known from past experience that friends weren't always the people you thought they were. Daniel and I had friends, or so I thought. However, things change. Divorce not only splits the couple apart but divides their friends between them, too. Friends I thought were mine, as well as Daniel's, disappeared along with my husband and my old life.

I realized that Sarah was standing, waiting for my answer with a look of innocence on her face. I couldn't erase the fun times we had shared, still, her lies hurt too much to share lunch with her and make small talk now. The fact that she tried covering up whatever secrets she had by belittling Betsy, hurt me even more than losing my friends back in Orlando. I had known them longer, like Barbara Anderson.

Daniel and I had Barbara and her husband over at least once a month. We used to throw elaborate dinner parties and they would come and enjoy the food and expensive wine. Looking back, being friends with Barbara was different from the friendship I thought I had with Sarah. I never formed a bond with Barbara like the one I had with Sarah. I guess that's why I was so hurt about Sarah being so secretive.

After the newspaper articles and police taking me in for questioning, all my so-called friends left. Barbara was the worst because she jumped at the opportunity to give an interview with a reporter from the newspaper. That's when I realized Barbara never cared about my poor Lily. Her only thought was to get her fifteen minutes of fame by exploiting the fact that she knew me. She hatefully told the reporter, "Stephanie Oliver doesn't know how to be a good mother. She should go to jail for life."

I guess you never know who your friends truly are until something awful happens. Wolves disguised as friends, like Barbara, and like Sarah.

"Well?" Sarah prompted. "How's about lunch?"

"I'm not hungry. Guess I'm too tired to be hungry," I added. "Would you mind if I went on home? I think most everything is cleaned up."

"Of course, it's okay. I appreciate everything you—and Betsy—have done for me." Sarah smiled sheepishly. A concerned look took over her face. "Is everything okay with you? You seem so quiet."

"Yes, I'm just tired."

Things weren't okay. I hoped that maybe our friendship could be saved, but I didn't believe it was possible. Thinking back, things fell into focus. Sarah never asked me about myself, not because she didn't want to pry, like Betsy. Sarah was always too busy talking about herself.

After what happened in my past, I thought I had become a better judge of people. In one day, Betsy rose above most everyone I ever knew. She was unique. Betsy proved there was still such a thing as trustworthiness and sincerity. When I picked Sarah to be my friend, I chose the wrong person.

I left the store and headed to Betsy's house. I wanted to let her know not to worry about the store or Sarah's secret. I wanted to assure Betsy that she could count on me.

My Visit with Betsy

When I arrived at Betsy's house, she was on her front porch watering plants. Dressed casually in a soft blue denim shirt and navy pedal-pushers, she still was radiant. As I pulled up in front, Betsy looked up and gave a friendly wave.

"I'm so glad you stopped," she called out to me. "Come on up on the porch."

Betsy and Joe's house was on several acres of farmland. Their porch looked like a photo spread for *House and Garden*. Betsy had the proverbial green thumb. She stood there surrounded by hanging pots of spider plants, Swedish ivy, and an assortment of geraniums in pinks and vibrant reds. The house was a good size. A two-story with quite a few bedrooms, but not on the grand scale of the Brewer home—my home, now.

Saying *my home* always seemed strange. When it went up for sale, the listing identified it as the "Brewer House." In these parts, that's how people recognize homes—by the names of the original families. As with old antiques, rich in history, the house still seemed like it belonged to Mabel Brewer and I felt more like a caretaker rather than the new owner.

When I got to the porch Betsy said, "Stephanie, sit down on the swing and relax. I'll get us a cool drink."

The best thing about Betsy's porch was the beautiful wooden swing that hung from two chains extending from the ceiling. Betsy told me that Joe built it so the two of them could sit together in the evenings after dinner

"It's so hot, isn't it?" she commented as I took a seat. "August is one of our hottest months. I'll be just a minute." Betsy hurried into the house still talking as she disappeared inside. "I want to hear how the cleanup went at the store."

With the focus on the fire at the store, thoughts about the hidden space in my living room closet had gotten pushed back into the background. I wanted Betsy's insight about the space I had found. I knew if anyone could bring some new light to the situation, it would be Betsy. I needed to find a way to work the subject of concealed spaces into the conversation. I thought over options while swinging. I didn't want to just blurt out; *I found a secret space in my house.*

The soft clicking sound of the swing with its slow rhythm, back and forth, had an almost hypnotic effect as I felt myself relax. *Maybe all the homes around here have secret spaces*, I thought. Thinking that was a silly thought, I quickly dismissed it. After all, if secret spaces were common than they wouldn't be a good place to hide something.

As Betsy mentioned, the day was a hot one. Still, the warm air felt good, soothing. Maybe it was just being here on Betsy's porch that made it a comfort. Everything about Betsy and Joe's home gave a pleasant, nice, and inviting feel. It felt welcoming and safe here.

"I wanted to call the store, but knew you'd be busy," Betsy said as she came out carrying a tray of tea sandwiches, cookies, and a pitcher of iced tea.

"I wish Sarah had let me come in today and help. I didn't want to insist because sometimes she can be *particular* about things. She can get a little grouchy if she feels she's being dismissed and her wishes are ignored." Betsy placed the tray on a small table a few feet in front of the swing and sat down. "I'm not meaning anything bad," she continued. "I can understand— Tony doesn't really listen to her sometimes. Not everyone can be as lucky to have what Joe and I have."

"Everything got cleaned up okay," I said. I wanted to ask her what secrets Sarah felt she needed to hide from me, but I stopped myself. I didn't want her to think the reason I came over was to pump her for information.

"I think I know what you mean about Sarah being particular," I said. "Today, I saw her in a different light. I guess I don't know Sarah as well as I thought. Anyway, I wanted to let you know that I'm sorry I gave you a hard time yesterday. I was caught off guard; I thought Sarah and I were friends. I forgot I'm her employee."

Betsy touched my hand, "Stephanie, Sarah does think of you as a friend. I know it. Not everyone can share things easily. We never know what goes on behind closed doors—nor should we."

The sandwiches hit the spot. I didn't realize how hungry I was by then. Betsy and I sat for a few minutes longer not talking, just enjoying the sunshine and the distant songbirds singing.

"Joe doesn't stop for lunch," Betsy said, breaking the silence. "He prefers to skip lunch so he can stop work early on in the day. We have an early dinner and that way we have time afterward to spend together in the evening."

She smiled at a yellow swallowtail butterfly fluttering past us on its way to one of the red geraniums. "This is nice, having a light snack," she said. "Normally I don't eat anything in the afternoon. I don't like to eat alone."

"Betsy, before everything happened yesterday, I was thinking I would like to find out more about Mabel Brewer. You know, because I own her house now," I said. Somehow, it seemed logical, even if I hadn't found the hidden things in the closet.

"I understand the Brewers were one of the oldest families in these parts, dating back a couple of hundred years. You were born here; do you know something about her family?"

"Oh, yes. They were quite a family in their heyday. I knew Mabel, well not really knew her. It's more like I knew of her family. She was a schoolteacher. She taught sixth grade, my father was one of her students. She taught right up into her seventies. I saw her around town, but I didn't have her as a teacher. Mrs. Dover was my sixth-grade teacher."

Betsy stopped and tilted her head up as if grasping a lost memory. Then her eyes focused back on me. A small smile came to her lips and she shrugged. "It's funny you asked me about Mabel because Leanne Thompson came to me shortly after she moved here, asking the same thing."

As Betsy spoke, I pulled up the mental image of Leanne standing in my living room holding the plate of cookies. I could hear her soft voice as she apologized for walking into my home unannounced. There she was with her blond hair pulled into a ponytail, dark hickory brown eyes with golden flecks popping like Fourth of July sparklers from beneath long black lashes. The poor girl being caught up with the emergency of a fire at the store, and still, she was concerned enough for me to soften the news by grabbing the plate of homemade cookies she had just baked. The smell of those cookies became back to me now. Vanilla and cinnamon.

I sipped my tea as Betsy told me about Leanne commenting about being interested in Mabel Brewer. I realized, after months of living in Havenridge. I could count on one hand the things I knew about my neighbor, Leanne Thompson. What I did know was that Leanne had moved to Havenridge about a year and a half before I did and she had never been married but not much more.

Betsy said that Leanne was an artist and worked from home doing work for magazines, designing book covers and album covers, and such. That's why I didn't see much of her since she didn't leave the house for work every day.

I realized that by shielding my past from everyone, I had isolated myself. Betsy knew more about my neighbor than I did. The most I knew was Leanne lived at the top of the hill, spoke in a southern accent, and made delicious cookies.

Betsy continued chatting about Leanne. She wondered what connection Leanne possibly could have to the old Brewer family.

I interrupted her rambling and asked, "Betsy, if Leanne came asking about Mabel Brewer, maybe she knew about her before moving here?"

Taking another tea sandwich, Betsy said, "I don't know about that, could be. Before she came to me, she asked Sarah questions about Miss Brewer. Sarah knew that I know most everyone here 'bouts, so Sarah suggested Leanne ask me."

"What kind of questions did Leanne ask?" I prompted.

"She asked me about all kinds of things. Like, what Miss Mabel's father did, and what kind of person he was like. Questions like that. Most of the stories about the town and the Brewers, I know from my father and what he told me about growing up in Havenridge. Back then, the Brewer family pretty much ruled the community."

A gentle breeze blew, which Betsy said was unusual for this time of year. It was so pleasant on her porch. Tranquil. I saw some birds in flight, probably on their way to neighboring peach orchards. It seemed as close to heaven as you could get.

"Did Leanne say why she wanted to know about the Brewers?"

There were so many unanswered questions. I needed to get answers. Maybe Betsy would help me unravel the past. Who knows what could be linked to the box I found hidden in my living room closet.

"She said that she knew old man Brewer was a man not to cross," Betsy answered. "But she never explained where or who she heard that from,"

"Did she find what she was looking for?"

"I guess. I helped her get some facts, dates, things like that from county records, and from Pastor Davis at the church. She didn't know how to go about finding out things. Since I worked for the sheriff a while back, I knew where to look, or if not, I know who to ask for help. I worked for six years in the records department, so I still have connections at the courthouse."

Betsy wasn't suspicious by nature, so she never asked about my motives as I continued raising more questions. "Where did Leanne live before she moved here? Why move here?"

I hoped Betsy had been nosy enough to ask Leanne questions. "Does she have any relatives in Havenridge?"

"No, she doesn't. She moved from somewhere else in Georgia. I think not far from here, but she never actually said."

"Really," I said, pretending to be barely interested. I picked up another tea sandwich so I wouldn't have to support the conversation, hoping Betsy would continue. And she did.

"I don't think Leanne's a real homebody. She talked about her mother only briefly. Leanne commented that she was more of a wanderer then her immediate family members that she was more like a distant uncle she had, which relatives spoke about unfavorably."

Betsy paused, and took a drink, then said. "Leanne said that she had surprised herself when she felt drawn here and bought that house on the hill. She told me it was the first house she ever owned. Although, she'd worked since age fifteen so she had the money to buy before, but instead, she spent most of her free time traveling. When I was going through files at the courthouse I saw she paid cash for her home."

"Umm, I've been thinking, Betsy," I said. "I want to organize a sort of record of the people who have lived in my house. You know, like the people and the history of the area in a sort of album."

The reality was that I wanted to unweave the mystery building around that hidden space in my living room closet and I needed an excuse for asking her for help. This seemed like a logical reason as any for digging around about the Brewers.

I continued, "I'm guessing that the courthouse would have many of the things I would need. Can you help me pull things together? Show me where to look, like you did with Leanne?

"Of course. It'll be fun, but you might get more information if you go straight to some of the older residents in the area. But then again, most folks won't be so eager to help, especially the older ones. They don't like talking about things that happened in the past. Don't want to *own up* to everything that went on around here. Unless they're made to feel important."

"I could explain about wanting to document about my house and say I needed their help."

"No. Better to keep that part between you and me at first. I'll take you to see some of the older folks, but I'll just say we're coming for a visit. Most people want to be selective with sharing the town's history."

Secret Papers

I was determined to go through the hidden items in my closet more thoroughly once I got home. As I drove home from Betsy's, I set up a plan of action in my mind.

First, I won't ever make the mistake of leaving my front door unlocked again.

Second, I'll keep everything, after I see what everything is, to myself and store it in the concealed space. After all, the secret space went undetected for years, so it certainly was secure.

Betsy was my best bet to start any digging for information. She knew the right people to talk to and with her at my side; they were more likely to share. Even so, Betsy probably knew more town history than she realized.

Entering my house and locking the front door behind me, I went upstairs to change into my trusty sky blue pants and a T-shirt. I hurried downstairs and darted to the closet. The tools still lay on the floor where I had left them in my rush to block Leanne from witnessing my discovery. I turned the flashlight on and reached inside the dark hole for an old wooden crate. I could see more things pushed in the back part of the crawl space.

One, two . . . no, there were four bundled items. I piled the bundle items on top and dragged the crate into the well-lit living room. Moving the four tied bundles to the floor, I peered in the crate and saw on top a large leather-bound book. Then I realized that it was a Bible. On the first page was the Brewer family tree drawn with artistic swirls. Beneath one branch was written *Mabel Louise Brewer*, in a perfect flowing script—*birth December 12, 1883.*

I put the Bible aside and dug into the crate for the other items. There were aged photographs of my house with groups of people gathered on the veranda. I found an assortment of other photographs that were taken somewhere other than Havenridge. I didn't recognize where. One, in particular, caught my eye, a woman in a wheelchair in front of an enormous brick building. There were assorted papers, with two wrapped in cloth. Unwrapping the cloth, I found the contents had been securely tied with string.

There was a large-sized box at the bottom of the crate. It contained books that looked like ledgers with monthly payments recorded in columns with the dollar amounts. The rows down the page had initials and names. G.L.A.-Hanna was first, next to the name was Doctor T. Greenwood, which repeated in most of the following rows. About a fourth of the way down was listed the name Josephine, and then, Dr. P. Cooper.

In the large box were two more bundles, also tied with string, which were letters. Amongst all the items was another book, but it wasn't a ledger, it looked like a journal or diary. It was handwritten, with dated entries. The first page read, "Property of Cain Syrus Brewer."

The Letters

I untied one of the bundles of letters. The envelopes had yellowed with age and some of their corners crumbled in my hands. Thumbing through all the stacks of letters, I noticed only two names were addressed on the envelopes—Cain Brewer and Hanna Brewer. Picking an envelope with Hanna's name on it, I opened it, pulled out the paper, and unfolded it. The letter was from Cain.

1883
Dearest Hanna,

I hope this reaches you in an improved state of health. I am not good at running the household. Things do not go smoothly when you are not here.

My only hope is my next visit will bring to me more encouraging thoughts of your return. You must try harder to work on achieving a state of good health that will result with the doctors allowing you to return home to Havenridge.

Respectfully your loving husband,
Cain Brewer

Hanna must have left Havenridge but why and for how long, I didn't know. Picking up the photographs from among the scattered papers, I studied one picture of some women on a veranda. There was no date on the back of the photo. The old-fashioned dresses and button-up shoes the women wore looked as if it could be the late 1800s.

I wonder if Hanna is one of these women. Could she be the one in the wheelchair?

I pulled out a letter that Hanna wrote to Cain. It read:

> *My loving husband,*
> *I do not know what to report to you about my progress. Dr. Greenwood said I am improving. However, the truth is I am still not sleeping.*
> *I am trying very hard to get well. I want to be a good wife. I know the reason I am here is my fault.*
> *I long to come home and take care of the house and be a proper wife again.*
>
> *Respectively your wife,*
> *Hanna*

I opened and read a few more letters. All were similar, written very formally and properly. Except for one that was signed by Hanna. It surprised me. The tone was so different. It was as if a completely different person had written it. It was hard to follow, and the handwriting was so sloppy, it seemed extremely fractured in thought. It was addressed only to "Cain" and it read:

> *Cain,*
> *It is cold here, but you know that. You prayed for the cold, hoping I would get the sickness and die.*

Your plans will not work. I told Dr. Greenwood that I pretended to be asleep when you came into my room late last night. I saw you talking to the nurse. You gave her poison to put in my food. Just like mother, I won't eat. She may be dead, but she whispers in my ear when I am sleeping. She tells me you talk to the devil.

Mabel is weak. The devil controls her, so he wants her to live.

Dr. Greenwood is fooled by you.

They bury the weak ones out back.

You cannot get me because I do not sleep. I will tell.

I visited Mabel in her bedroom last night. Maybe tomorrow she will go to sleep and not wake up.

You cannot get me because God talks to me and tells me about you.

Liar, liar, liar, liar, liar, li . . .

I put the letter down. With each new piece that I discover, the image I had of Hanna became more blurred and confusing. This Hanna, who wrote, was hateful and suspicious. Worlds apart from the submissive and obedient Hanna in the other letter who wanted to come home "to be a good wife."

What in heaven's name was going on in this family?

I picked up Cain's journal and searched for entry dates close to the letters marked with dates and Hanna's bizarre letter.

There was nothing sinister in his words.

***

CAIN'S JOURNAL

December 3, 1884 – I received a letter from Dr. Greenwood. He stated no improvement in Hanna's condition. She is still not eating nor sleeping through the night. Nurses report her talking and arguing with herself into the early hours before sunrise. I fear the worst.

December 13, 1884 – Hanna is slipping away, mentally and physically, little-by-little each day. Dr. Greenwood last wrote that if she does not eat in the next few days that he will have to force food in her.

December 22, 1884 — I rode to the hospital today. It takes hours because the roads are not good and the distance is far. The bad weather makes it even more difficult. I wish I could travel to see Hanna more often. However, until traveling conditions improve I will have to make do with once a month.

When I arrived at the hospital, the nurses informed me that Hanna had started eating again. Hanna was happy to see me and begged to come home. She misses Mabel. The doctors warned me that if my wife returns home and has another spell that Mabel's safety could be in jeopardy. I am afraid I will not have my dear Hanna home ever again. I fear she is like Josephine.

I looked at another stack of letters. They were addressed to Mabel but had never been opened. The handwriting was, without a doubt, different from any of the other letters I had seen. There was no sender's name or address on the envelopes. The mystery of the Brewer family swelled with every item I touched.

Tomorrow, Betsy and I are going to visit one of the "older folks," as Betsy refers to him. I hope the visit will help shed some light on the bewildering people in these letters.

Clarence Swain

Today Betsy would take me to meet Clarence Swain. She said he is the last person in Havenridge left living who had grown up with Mabel. He would know more facts about the Brewer family than anyone she knew. The day at the store seemed to drag on, waiting for the time to go meet Clarence. I was anxious to speak to one of the elders of the town.

Sarah said I could leave ten minutes early when I asked her this morning. It was getting about time for me to leave when I heard the bell over the store's front door jingle.

"Oh, it's Miss Gladys," Sarah said. "You need to stay a few more minutes to meet her."

"Okay," I said. I didn't want to stay but couldn't refuse.

"She's from the church auxiliary," Sarah continued. "She stops in regularly to pick up supplies for the church's after-service get-togethers. I'm surprised you haven't met her yet."

Sarah introduced us.

"How do you do," Miss Gladys said while extending a white-gloved hand.

She was a plump lady wearing a cotton shirtwaist dress with a printed pattern of small violets and pearl buttons down the front. She put her purse down and pulled out a handwritten list of only three items on it. Coffee, cookies, and tea napkins. I figure it wouldn't take too long to complete business. Still, she chatted away about all the comings and goings of the church. She informed me of her duties in the church office, which of course she carried out flawlessly, in her opinion. Twenty minutes later, I knew everything about Gladys. How she maintained the church's linen tablecloths, starching and ironing them to perfection every Saturday for the last fifteen years along with more info I didn't need to know.

"Before I took over the job," Gladys said, "Mildred Smith was in charge. She used to put wrinkled tablecloths down on Sunday mornings. I explained to Mildred that wrinkled tablecloths were not the proper way for hosting church gatherings, nor was it very reverent."

Gladys paused and straightened her dress. "Mildred rarely comes to church anymore. She only comes on Palm Sunday, Easter, and Christmas," she said rolling her eyes. "I knew she wasn't very devout, I think she only comes to show off her new dresses."

I started to bag her items, hoping to rush her along. "Do you want me to put this on the church's account?"

"Yes, thank you, my dear."

"It was a pleasure meeting you, Miss Gladys. Thank you."

Gladys took the bag and before she left, she turned to me and said, "You should come to our Sunday service, dear. It is at nine o'clock sharp, and coffee and cookies are served directly afterward."

"Thank you, I'll try to make it."

Don't hold your breath, you old bitty, I thought. *I suppose if I came wearing the wrong dress—one too new or too bright in color, or maybe even wrinkled, you would make me feel as welcome as poor Mildred Smith. No wonder the poor thing only goes to church three times a year.*

After Miss Gladys left, I gathered my things and said goodbye to Sarah. Even with my delay, I wouldn't be late since I had planned to leave the store early.

I arrived at two-forty and saw Betsy waiting on her porch swing. I waved and pulled in the driveway. She hurried to the car, got in, and started talking right away. "It should take around thirty minutes to get to the old farmhouse. He used to grow cotton, but not on the scale that old man Brewer's land produced. Clarence must be in his nineties now and doesn't work the farm anymore. I know he sectioned off part of his land a few years ago and sold several acres. I saw the paperwork when I worked in the courthouse. He knew Mabel, but I don't know how well. He was a few years younger than she was. Of course, everyone knew the Brewers. My father said he always heard that Clarence was more connected with the Brewers' history because their families competed for cotton money."

"What reason did you give him for my visit?" I asked.

"Oh, you'll like this, Stephanie. I told him you're writing a book on the history of Havenridge and some of the people who live here. You know if people think you're going to write about them, they're more willing to talk to you. The trick will be getting him to stop talking about himself and tell us about the Brewers. My father used to say there were rumors about a big-time feud between the Swains and the Brewers. Clarence would never have agreed to talk to us if he knew it was about the Brewers. I hate not being honest. However, sometimes the good Lord understands about white lies."

We passed peach orchards, and then a field of either cotton or young tobacco plants. I can't tell the difference between them, yet. Then shortly afterward, I saw the old frame house. Betsy said it looked in worse condition than she remembered.

The last time she and Joe had been there was after a big storm had passed through. It left most people on the outskirts of town in need of help.

"Joe and I didn't know if Clarence had electricity in his house, and if he did, we figured he had probably lost power. A lot of people were out of power for weeks after that big storm and most didn't have generators. People around Havenridge wouldn't spend money on a generator just for lights and the farms didn't need electricity to keep operating like the big dairy farms with milking machines. Some old-timers still used kerosene lamps," Betsy said.

"Once we were able to get over to check on Clarence, we did, but it was 'bout a week and a half after the storm. Clarence's electricity was back on when we got there. Clarence said that he had his house 'modernized,' as he put it, years earlier. He was okay. Nevertheless, it was a good thing we went over to check on him. With his power off, his food had spoiled and he would've eaten it. He can't smell—never could. He was born without a sense of smell. The stench about knocked me over when I opened the refrigerator."

"We restocked food for him and fixed some things around the place. He has no one to help him—no family. He's not a bad, old man, but he's not that nice. He'll tell you off as easily as say good morning to you. He doesn't worry about hurting anybody's feelings. Everyone in town leaves him alone."

"Sounds like a gem, if you ask me," I said.

Betsy gave an understanding smile. "Joe and I feel sorry for him—but he is a mean old buzzard, that's for sure."

We parked out in front and headed up the steps of the old farmhouse.

Writing a book, that would be interesting. I never thought of writing a book. Havenridge has enough strange characters and enough mysteries beneath the surface, I could write two or three books.

Clarence and Mabel

The house was medium in size. It appeared to have been built small with parts added on, doubling the original size. In a chair on the wraparound porch sat a man with snowy-white hair and sun-beaten skin that resembled a worn piece of rawhide.

"Hello, Clarence," Betsy called out.

He looked up and scowled, not saying a word.

"Betsy, he knew we were coming today, didn't he?" I asked.

"Oh yes, I told you he's a different type of person," Betsy whispered as we approached the porch. "You won't see him smile. I don't think I ever have, not even when we restocked his food and helped him with those repairs. And he'll never say thank you. I think it hurts him. It's as if he's admitting he needs help. He's used to being in charge. I don't think he had an easy life, probably had to fight for everything. Maybe he can't get out of the arguing mode."

Even as we stepped up on the porch, he kept frowning. Betsy did the introductions and our visit started with some small talk. Betsy sure had him pegged. I sat quietly as she told him what was going on in town, and then she asked him about his arthritis pain.

"What do you know about arthritis? You're young," he barked his response. "You get old and your bones hurt. That's how you know you're still alive. It's part of life—that is if hard work is part of your life. Young people don't know what it's like to work hard. You don't know. Farm work, that's hard work."

"Now, Clarence, you know Joe and I know what farm work is like. Remember years past, we had to take care of Mr. Wilcox's farm and my folks' land, both. You remember Mr. and Mrs. Wilcox; Joe's folks. They grew tobacco and my parents had the farm down the road. My dad, Leslie Barret, went to school with your son."

"I remember Leslie. I went to grammar school with his dad, your grandfather. I only finished the eighth grade and then had to quit to work the farm. Your granddad finished twelve years of school and went off for two years of college over in Baldwin County. He made some good money, came back in his fancy clothes, and bought his farm where you live now. He had an easy life—didn't know hard times. You betcha, I remember. Do you think I'm senile? I remember all the families from 'round here," he growled at sweet Betsy.

"That's why we're here, Clarence. Stephanie here is gathering information about Havenridge and the people for her book. You know just about everything 'round about these parts. You ran your farm," Betsy turned to me and said, "It was one of the best cotton farms in the county."

"*One* of the best? Why it would've been *the* best—that is if it hadn't been for all of the double-crossing deals of Cain Brewer. Never could trust him. Out to get all he could swindle out of a person. Took after his namesake from the Bible. No good, both Cains."

"Did you know Stephanie bought the old Brewer house?"

"She did?" he said, glancing at me with a frown and a suspicious look, not softening any.

"Yes, Mr. Swain," I said, thinking that this was my chance to jump in and ask him some questions. "I understand Mabel Brewer passed away a few years ago. I guess she was Cain Brewer's daughter. Did you know Mabel?"

"Yes. Mabel was a pretty thing," he said. A hint of a smile formed on the rock-hard face of the old man. Then it quickly disappeared. His face froze as a far-away look took over in his eyes. "Sweet, too—not like her father. I guess she took after her mother. Maybe that's why her father could control her so. He ruined her life. Just the same way as he did his poor wife, I take it. Heard Mabel's mother was kinda' . . . . delicate. Talk was she had a *nervous* condition. But I don't know for sure. Never saw her, 'cause she didn't live here."

This coarse old man had so many contradictive sides to him. When he spoke of Mabel, you could feel the tenderness in his voice, like the sweet magnolia-scent in the air. Any other time he was rough as sandpaper. I guess that tenderness was the hidden side of Clarence that Betsy's natural intuitiveness sensed.

"What was Mabel like?" I asked carefully. "I'm told that she never got married."

"Oh, Mabel was pretty as a picture. Every boy in town wanted to court her. Most were afraid to because of Old Man Brewer. I told my dad I wanted to go callin' for her and he warned me. '*Don't you pay no attention to Cain Brewer,*' he told me. '*You talk to Mabel. Don't bother asking permission to call on her from that miserable man. If he has his way poor Mabel will be an old maid.*' I did what dad said. She and I would meet at Blue Lake. She wasn't pushed around by her father back then, when she was young, that is. He hadn't broken her spirit, yet."

"So Mabel was your girlfriend?" I asked.

"Girlfriend? Well, I guess she was my girlfriend for a while. But it was different back then. You couldn't call someone your girlfriend until you had the family's blessing, and then, that only meant you could come to Sunday supper. Couples couldn't see each other alone. That's why I said Mabel was different. Meeting me at the lake like that. It was very daring, you know. Spunky. If anyone had known, there would've been all kinds of talk. Just the same, she remained a lady. There was no hanky-panky."

"What happened with you and her?" I asked. "Did the two of you ever think of getting married?"

"I would've asked her, but then a drifter came into town. She told me she had fallen in love with someone and couldn't see me anymore. Mabel never told me it was him, but I knew. Rumors were going around like wildfire about the young man living in the abandoned shack on the outskirts of town."

"What was his name? Do you know where he came from?" I asked.

Suddenly the air went icy and Clarence's scowl came back harder than ever.

"You sure ask a lot of questions. It's town business and your family isn't even from these parts. Hell, townsfolk didn't even know Mabel was meetin' me. It wasn't their business and it's not yours," he said. His face was red with irritation.

Oh, now I've ruined it. He probably knows more than anyone around here. And now he's furious.

"Now Clarence, don't be that way," Betsy's voice warmed the icy air. "You know me. I wouldn't bring a nosy outsider here to snoop. Remember, when we were young and sometimes forgot our manners? Stephanie is young and has never heard the old stories of the interesting people of these parts. That's why she wants to write about Havenridge. She wanted to document things about the Brewer house and I asked, *why write only about the Brewers?* I told her your family had been here just as long as they had been and grew cotton, too. Why you probably have more stories to tell than she'd have room for in her book."

"Well, for sure," he said. The tension left his face. "Why, we owned eighty acres of rich cotton land."

Betsy was brilliant. He sat there rocking and I kept my mouth shut. I glanced over at Betsy. She smiled back at me, as she patiently fanned herself with a piece of paper she had retrieved from her purse.

After a few agonizing minutes of silence Clarence continued, "Yes, Mabel was pretty as a picture." His face softened and a tranquil smile rolled in again. He started to speak as if we weren't there, more like reminiscing to himself. "I would've married her even if old man Brewer threatened me. After she stopped seeing me, people around town all said she was planning to run away with that drifter. I think his name was John or Jack."

"Jacob. Could it have been Jacob?" I blurted out before I realized.

Clarence gave a quick glance in my direction. "Maybe, it was something like that, but then he went missin'. After that, Mabel changed. She didn't go against her father anymore. She turned into the dutiful daughter and the old maid that her father wanted her to be."

The rest of the afternoon Clarence's reminiscing flowed like a steady current of water. I only hoped I could remember all the names he spoke of in his stories. I let Betsy do most of the talking after that. I didn't want to get Clarence angry again. I watched in awe at Betsy's gentle and comforting way she interacted with this prickly old man.

After about two hours, Betsy thanked him, saying that we needed to leave because Joe would be finishing up out in the field. Before leaving she said, "Clarence, can Stephanie and I come again to hear some more of your stories about the town and your life on the farm? We *so* enjoyed today."

"Yep, if you want to. Ain't much to tell, though. I worked the farm until I got too old. Now all I do is read my Bible and wait for the good Lord to call me home. I got plenty of time for storytelling."

Family Records

As I drove away with Betsy, I saw Clarence pick up a book, probably his Bible, and start reading.

"Wow, he sure has a lot of stories. You think they're all true?"

"Oh, I'm sure they're true," said Betsy. "I'm also sure he's holding back the majority of the details. The carryings-on of the past is what the older folks around here want to keep to themselves. Things that probably aren't so pretty or respectable—and believe me, he knows all of them."

"You think he and Mabel really did sneak off to Blue Lake? Maybe some hanky-panky did go on."

"Hanky-panky? Probably not, remember that was over eighty years ago. Just sneaking off without a chaperone was risqué. They both had the whole town to face and their families too if caught. But a drifter . . . that would be a different story. He wouldn't care about town gossip. That's where the story is hidden, Stephanie. I'd bet my life on it.

"Mabel Brewer was a unique person from what my father told me," Betsy said. "She taught my dad, but his description was so much different from what we heard today."

"Different? In what way?"

"Well, remember, Dad knew her as his teacher. You know kids never think their teachers have a life outside of the classroom. They certainly can't imagine them dating, let alone, sneaking off to the woods to meet a beau. When she was Dad's teacher, she was only in her middle sixties. He said she was the type of person who gave the air of being elderly, even back then. That was also my impression when I was a little girl and I would see her in town. She always carried herself with the steadiness of a much older, prim, and proper lady."

"I know what you mean. I think everybody knows someone like that," I said. "When I was growing up, the lady down the street was the same way. I thought of her as really old. Several years later, sometime after I had graduated from high school my mom told me that the lady took early retirement at age sixty-two. So that meant she was only in her late thirties or early forties when I was a little girl."

Betsy nodded in agreement. "Exactly my point. And Dad said no one ever called Mabel by her first name. Not even people her own age. The children in her classroom were expected to conduct themselves with proper manners and address her as *Miss Brewer*. According to Dad, she said that *a lady never stands for the familiarity of being addressed by her first name*. When you think about it, it's strange she turned so proper. Who would have guessed she had a secret lover."

While Betsy spoke, I pictured in my mind two very different Mabels. The first one, the young one, who had been pretty and free-spirited with hopes and dreams ahead of her—the woman Clarence had known. The second Mabel, the changed one, who was the well-behaved, respectful, and submissive one. The latter one would remain forever. Mabel's life had stopped in time, waiting for a lover that never returned and living a long life of ninety-eight-years, and no doubt, most of those years very lonely.

"Boy, so many images of one person. I guess what's real is only how one perceives the situation or person," I said.

107

"You're right. When or why Mabel lost her youthfulness was never quite clear—until now," Betsy said. "I grew up hearing rumors of a boyfriend when she was young, but we never believed it. We all knew the tales about him living alone, a few miles outside of town. Stories were that he did handiwork for money or in trade for food and grew vegetables on the land. There was even legend of coded love letters the drifter wrote to Mabel. Crazy stories that kids swear are true. The tales went that one day the drifter disappeared and later on his letters stopped coming. The grandparents of some friends of mine swore that Mabel kept his picture and spoke about him, saying he came one night to tell her he would return for her. After I grew up, I dismissed the stories. I figured they were fabricated from the wild imagination of kids in a small town with nothing better to do. Now I'm not so sure about it, after hearing Clarence's story."

"How could someone disappear and no one investigate?" I asked.

"It was the turn of the century, Stephanie. Remember Clarence said the guy was a drifter and nobody knew much about him. He probably didn't have any family. I guess back then people would come to a town and take squatter's rights of abandoned houses. I know there are still a few houses outside of town hidden by overgrown brush. Any evidence that anyone inhabited them would be buried inside. There's one not far from your place that's swallowed up by wisteria vines covering almost the entire house. Anyone driving by wouldn't have a clue that something would be under there."

Clarence's conversation gave me a zest to find out more. I wanted to learn everything about Mabel and her whole family. My enthusiasm bubbled inside of me.

"What's our next move, Betsy? Where can we get more information about the Brewer family?"

"Well, I can try to find records at the courthouse. I know there are deed records of the land. That should give us the name of Cain's father. If we can get a few names, we can start looking at birth, death, and marriage records. Though, we may have to send a request for those to the capital. It's going to take time," Betsy said. "We're starting with nothing but Mabel and Cain Brewer's names."

I thought about the hidden stash in the closet back at the house. I reconsidered telling Betsy about what I'd found, at least, sharing about the pictures. Betsy certainly could be trusted with a secret. Clarence might recognize some of the people in the photos. Still, I wanted to keep the letters and the journal to myself for a little while longer. *Maybe some of the letters are from Mabel's mysterious drifter.* I needed to check.

"Betsy, I found some things that belonged to the Brewers. At least, I think they belonged to them. They were packed away in the house. Some pictures and a Bible."

"Stephanie, you found a Bible? A family Bible?"

"Well, yes, I guess it's a family Bible. What would make it a family Bible?"

"Well, they're usually bigger than most Bibles you would find today," Betsy answered.

"The one I found is big. Maybe the size of typewriter paper or bigger."

Betsy's eyes sparkled and she spoke fast with excitement. "Stephanie, this part of the country is the Bible Belt. People around here are very religious and take their Bibles seriously. The Bible was, and still is for most folks, the center of everything," she explained. "Years ago, families were ruled by one person, the head of the household, usually the father but sometimes a grandfather. Always an elder of the family, and always a man. Wives weren't part of any decision-making. Back then, they based everything on the word of the gospel. All the family records were entered into the family Bible. Births, marriages, deaths, everything. Remember back then, people didn't go to hospitals to have babies. They gave birth at home. And when someone died, the wake was held at home, with the body of the deceased laid out for viewing in the parlor. Stephanie, if you have the Brewer Family Bible, you have a gold mine. Weeks, maybe months of research probably wouldn't uncover half of what could be recorded in that Bible."

I grew up only a few hours from Georgia, but the people and customs were worlds from what I recognized. I came from a medium-size town, certainly not a big metropolitan city, but so different. How could I've been so stupid? What I had hidden away might disclose a history of generations.

"I'll check the Bible when I get home. Where do people record things in their family Bibles?"

"The ones I've seen, it's usually on the first few pages in the front. I guess it could be anywhere. If they ran out of room, they'd write on loose paper, fold it, and place it inside the Bible."

I turned into Betsy's driveway. Joe was out front on the porch swing. He waved and headed toward the car. I rolled the window down to greet him.

"Hi, Stephanie. So how'd it go with Clarence?" Joe asked. "That old geezer sure is a character, isn't he?"

"Yeah, Clarence is different, that's for sure, but he knows a lot. That's if he wants to tell you. You should've been there, Joe. Betsy was great. She knew just how to handle him. I wouldn't have ever gotten him to even talk to me if she hadn't been there."

"That's my Betsy, she can charm the honey from bees," Joe said. He looked over at Betsy. "Hi, honey. I quit a little early. I knew you girls would be late, so I put the pot roast in the big black pot and turned the stove on low. It'll be ready in about forty-five minutes. I thought maybe we could drive over to Blue Lake before dinner."

Joe looked at me and offered an explanation. "It's really a pretty spot, Stephanie. It's tucked away. You have to go on a small path through a wooded area and then there's a little clearing that opens up to the most beautiful lake. It's not too far from your house, just a short walk from your front door. Only the locals know about it. Maybe you'd like to join us. Have you ever been there?"

"No, I haven't. Although, I've heard about it. Thanks, Joe, I need to head home. I have some reading to do. Anyway, from what I've heard Blue Lake is more for couples," I said and gave a wink to Betsy.

"I'll check on what we talked about, Betsy. I'll call or stop over tomorrow after work. Thanks again for helping me. I'll see you."

Betsy and Joe said goodbye to me. As I drove away, I looked in the rearview mirror and saw them walking off with arms wrapped around each other's waist.

I would find out soon that while Betsy and I were out at Clarence's someone was driving from Orlando to my house. A surprise I had hoped to avoid a bit longer.

Unexpected Visitor

His plan had been not to call me, just get in his car and come. That way I wouldn't have the opportunity to talk him out of coming. His concern for me had escalated during the last five months. He feared that my abrupt decision to move was a sign of a person at the beginning stages of unraveling. He had ignored his worries and stayed away too long.

Unfortunately, for me, I had described the Brewer house to him so vividly that he would be able to pick my house out without any directions. Everything I told him was dead on, right down to the split in the road. Here's what I learned from him about the time he spent before I returned home.

***

He pulled into my driveway and saw the house numbers by the front door. Turning the ignition off, he noticed my car wasn't there. He gazed at the massive house in front of him. "Wow, what a house. Well, you never do anything ordinary do you, my lady."

After putting his bag on the porch, he decided to walk to the small house up on the hill. Maybe the neighbor there would have some information on my whereabouts.

The walk took only five minutes. The house was freshly painted. Nestled in the surrounding garden was a hand-painted welcome sign right between a spider jasmine bush and an enormous blue hydrangea. At the screen door, a nameplate hung with similar hand lettering which read *Thompson Residence*. Jazz music played inside and the lively sound drifted out onto the porch.

The man called through the screen door. "Hello, is anyone home?"

"Yes, I'll be right there. Just a minute."

The interior door sat open, leaving way for him to see a woman's silhouette coming down the hall. She walked with a bounce that made her ponytail sway from side to side.

"I'm sorry to bother you. I came to visit my sister, Stephanie—"

"You're Stephanie's brother," she interrupted and opened the screen door wide. "Come in, I didn't know Stephanie had a brother. Well, I mean . . . I don't know Stephanie that well. We've talked, but just small talk." She extended her hand as she introduced herself. "I'm Leanne Thompson."

"I'm Steve Gregory. Stephanie does live in the house at the bottom of the hill, doesn't she? I wasn't sure if I had the right house."

"Oh yes, that's her house. Isn't she home?" she asked. "I bet she's at Betsy's. She usually stops there after work. Ever since the fire . . . ."

"Fire, what fire? Is she okay?"

"She's okay. I'm sorry to have alarmed you. I assumed you knew about the fire. It was at the store where she works. It was a small fire. I mean the building didn't catch fire. Just some towels."

"Well, I've been on the road a lot lately. I haven't talked to Steph for a while. I didn't let her know I was coming."

"She doesn't come home early anymore," Leanne said. "I asked her if she had changed her work hours because I go outside to water the garden around four o'clock and normally her car is in the driveway by then. She told me that she and Betsy have been getting together in the afternoons. I'm afraid sometimes Stephanie's not home until close to five or six."

He was embarrassed as he realized how much of his sister's new life had been kept from him. She had intentionally kept details of her life in Havenridge from him and that was not normal. This beautiful stranger even knew what time Stephanie came home from work. He hadn't even known she had a job.

Embarrassed, he realized he was babbling excuses of not knowing exactly which house belonged to his one and only sister.

The captivating woman smiled. "I was painting some vines around the top of the walls in my kitchen when you called out. Why don't you come on back to the kitchen while I clean my brushes?"

He followed her down the hallway to the kitchen like a little puppy.

"Would you like a cold drink? I can call Betsy if you want to see if Stephanie is there."

"No—I mean don't call Betsy's house, and yes, uh, a drink sounds great. Tea or just water would be good."

Upon entering the kitchen, things went downhill from there. He lost all ability to speak in a coherent manner. Perhaps it was Leanne's bewitching brown eyes that turned the normally charming and debonair man into a bumbling idiot.

In the kitchen, her artistic talent was obvious to Steve. Traveling around the top of the four walls were vines weaving in and out of a flowing script, which read:

Feel the beauty

Hear the music

Nourish the soul

Live . . . Laugh . . . Love

"Oh, my . . . uh . . . is this . . . did you paint this? Oh, of course, you did, you have a paintbrush in your hand."

Leanne blushed, smiled, and answered in a soft and low, almost angelic voice, "Yes."

There were orchids, morning glories, lilies of the valley, and wisteria, with the occasional butterfly here and there. The flowers, vines, and the words intertwined together.

A few years back Steve had collaborated with a botanist to produce a reference book. He took the photos of hundreds of plants and helped the editor with the indexing. It took hours and hours of work. However, he walked away from the experience with the knowledge of flowers, and the intricate differences of each petal and leaf of many species. On this small kitchen wall, every painted petal and leaf were incredibly accurate. Leanne's detail was so realistic and amazing it left him breathless; as did the beautiful artist that he had just met.

A Surprise Homecoming

When I arrived home, I saw the unfamiliar flashy, metallic silver car. *What in the world? I don't know anyone who owns a Jaguar.*

It was certain that no one around this country town would own a luxury sports car like the one parked in front of my house. The license plate was from Orange County. *Oh, no. Could someone from Orlando have tracked me to Havenridge?*

The car was empty and no one was sitting in the wicker chair on the porch. I got out and looked around. I put my hand on the hood of the car. It was cool. I wasn't in any mood to have a visitor or have to deal with a nosy reporter today. Moving to Havenridge marked the end of my defending myself to others. My mind whirled with the possibilities of what or who lay ahead, waiting to ambush me. Whoever it was, I hoped that they hadn't stopped in town for directions.

When I got to the porch, I saw my brother's beat-up duffle bag. Relief washed over me. *Thank goodness. It's Steve. I should've known I couldn't put off his visit for long.*

I turned and looked at the Jag in the driveway. "He complains about me not communicating," I said out loud. "What about him? Buying a new car and not telling me."

I unlocked the front door and took another look around outside before going into my house. *I wonder where he went. I hope he didn't go snooping too far away.*

I went upstairs to change into comfortable clothes. When I returned downstairs, I put water on for tea and stepped out to the porch to get his duffle bag. That's when I saw them, Steve and Leanne walking down the hill toward me. They were talking and laughing as if they were old friends. It was anyone's guess what was in store for me.

I went back inside, turned off the teakettle, and sat down to wait. I felt like a prisoner counting down time on death row. The few minutes' wait seemed like an eternity. Then Steve's comforting voice called through the screen door.

"Steph, it's me. We saw your car pull up. Leanne is with me."

Somehow, no matter what the situation, hearing Steve's voice always lifted any weight I was carrying and made life seem bearable again.

"Come in," I called out as I went to meet them at the door. "Why didn't you tell me you were coming?"

I was glad he was here and started to cry when I hugged him. I didn't care if he would be mad at me about keeping my past a secret from everyone here. I didn't care about anything now. My brother was here and all I knew was when he was around I felt safe and life didn't hurt so much.

"Steph, why are you crying?" His eyebrows furrowed in concern.

"I'm just happy to see you. I'm being a girl, okay?"

I patted my eyes dry and looked at Leanne. I wasn't going to worry about what Steve might have said to her. I was happy that someone in my new life had met my brother.

"Leanne, I take it you two have gotten acquainted?"

Smiling, Leanne looked over, her eyes sparkling with an intense focus on Steve. Her soft voice she answered, "Oh, yes."

I turned, looked at Steve, then at her, and then back at Steve. His grin was a repeat of the one he'd flashed when I had walked in and caught him kissing Linda Clarke when he was fifteen.

"When did you get here? Were you at Leanne's waiting for me very long?"

"No, not long," they said in unison.

"I got here about three-thirty. What time is it now?"

"Six-twenty."

"Oh really," he said. Steve glanced at Leanne with an impish grin and a twinkle in his eye, as if they shared some secret information not privy to anyone else.

Smiling and blushing slightly, Leanne shrugged and said, "Well, I guess I'd better go so you can visit with your sister."

"You don't have to go, Leanne," I said. "Why don't you stay and have something to eat with us?"

"Thanks, but I know you two have lots of catching up to do. I don't want to intrude. Anyway, I need to finish cleaning up some paint things that I left out in the kitchen."

Before I could insist she wouldn't be intruding, Steve offered to walk her to the door. When he said goodbye, I heard him tell her he'd call her before he left.

Well, now that's interesting. I guess whether I like it or not, it looks like Leanne will be getting to know my family.

After he returned I said, "Steve, we have to talk."

"Yes, Stephanie, we do."

My brother only called me Stephanie when he was really worried. I knew the talk would be serious. I would have to convince him that I needed to bury my past along with all the police accusations. That night we had a long talk. Steve spoke about meeting Leanne and I realized one interesting thing, the

118

unattached artist and neighbor of mine had worked her way into my brother's heart.

Thinking about the last few months, I realized another thing, I hadn't been fair keeping my brother at a distance. I needed to let him back into my life.

My Confession to Steve

Steve and I stayed up talking past two-thirty, but when I woke the next morning I wasn't even the slightest bit tired. When I went downstairs to make coffee and passed the guestroom door, I heard him moving around inside. Last night Steve made me promise I'd think about sharing my past with someone here. Steve insisted that holding onto secrets was a heavy burden. I knew he was right, so I said I would think about it. I had already thought about sharing some things with Betsy yesterday, but we had been so involved with talking to Clarence that the right moment had not presented itself.

Steve had always been a straightforward kind of person. He hated secrets. I trusted him to be my rock and be there for me whenever Daniel wasn't. When I left Orlando, I had hidden from Steve how deeply depressed I had gotten, and yes, even suicidal. My brother had been an uncle, friend, and fill-in daddy for my daughter when Daniel was globetrotting and teaching the up-and-coming doctors of the future. The way I saw it, Steve had been my strength. If I was ever to become independent and survive, I needed to stand on my own two feet. My self-imposed exile from my brother had been for him as much as for me.

Hitting rock bottom and moving away I thought had been only about me. I never realized that during those dark moments without my beautiful Lily and those tragic days of my life had affected my brother, too. Last night's sister-brother talk opened my eyes.

Steve was the one everyone relied on, he always supported others who were hurting. I'd never known him to lean on anyone. It surprised me that he spoke to Leanne about his concerns about my mental state. I understood it was not a betrayal. My strong brother was human—he needed support, too. Leanne assured him that I wasn't alone as long she was next door. She would be only a call away for me, or him. Thinking about everything we talked about last night, I thought that Leanne must be quite a person. I don't remember Steve ever being that connected to any of his past girlfriends.

I opened the refrigerator to see if I had anything to offer for breakfast and shuffled around foil-wrapped leftovers. *Maybe I have a carton of eggs in here.*

"Hi, Steph. What a beautiful day!"

Startled to hear Steve's voice behind me, I jumped and bumped my head on the edge of the freezer door.

"Ouch," I said, rubbing the top of my head. "You're awfully peppy so early in the morning. What's this about? You never liked the mornings. You were always grumpy."

"Yeah, I'm not a morning person, but neither are you. Look at you, Steph, you're up, even dressed, and coffee's on. I guess it's due to good country living. You know, Orlando has changed a lot in the last ten years. After Disney World moved in, it's getting more . . . well, big city. Maybe you moving here wasn't a bad idea. Listen—the birds are singing. That's nice to hear—birds singing."

I stared at my brother, hardly recognizing the morning-loving mutation in front of me. "I think your sunny mood has more to do with a certain blond-haired neighbor of mine."

"Maybe," he said as one of his impish grins begun to spread across his face.

The rest of the morning we visited and then around eleven o'clock I suggested a drive. I took Steve on a tour of the town and surrounding area. We returned home to prepare lunch. While in the kitchen fixing sandwiches, I took the opportunity to tell him about the letters in my closet.

"Steve, you know the woman who owned this house before I bought it lived here all her life. She died at ninety-eight years old."

"You're not going to tell me the place is haunted, are you?"

"No, but she did leave some things behind. That is, someone in the Brewer family did. I found some letters, a journal and some pictures. I think they belonged to her father and I'm not sure if Mabel even knew about them."

"Mabel? Now you're on a first-name basis with this dead woman?"

"Stop it and listen, I'm serious. Mabel Brewer and her family lived in this house. In fact, they built it. The Brewers were powerful people here. At least her father had a lot of influence and wealth. I guess he was something like a Howard Hughes of these parts. His name was Cain. I've heard he strong-armed many people. Anyway, I found this hidden space in the back of a closet with all kinds of papers and things."

"Yeah, did you find some money?" Steve said as he poured a cup of coffee.

"Nah. But there's more. I want to show you the stuff before you leave. I intend to find out more about this Cain Brewer, and about Mabel. My friend Betsy is helping me. The Brewer family has a story and secrets, maybe important ones. Who knows what but there's a lot of history buried here and I'm going to get to the bottom of it."

Sarah's Dessert

When I had called Sarah to tell her my brother was in town and I wanted to switch shifts with her she was so excited. Of course she said it was okay with her to come in later and close the store. She asked me to bring Steve into the store at noontime for her to meet him. I explained he had to be on the road by then because he had a full day of travel to get to the town he had booked for a photo shoot the next day. After some diplomatic maneuvers, Sarah accepted my excuse that there wasn't enough time for them to meet.

I was getting pretty good at disguising things to work in my favor and only sharing what I wanted. Sarah said that she wanted to hear all about Steve's visit and insisted on coming to my house with a late-night dessert after I closed the store.

"We can do some catching up," Sarah said. "I'll put the girls to bed early and read a bedtime story to them then I can come over. I don't get to spend time with them in the evenings normally since I usually close the store most nights. It'll be a treat." She continued rambling on like only Sarah can do, effortlessly and without end. "Most nights Tony is deep into drafting a job by the time I get home. The few times I am home early, he still goes into the den and starts working right after the girls go to bed. I guess he can't break the habit."

I was glad Sarah insisted on coming over. I did miss visiting with her, even though I felt a lot closer to Betsy since the fire and Sarah's lying episode. When I first met Sarah, we had instantly clicked. We seemed to react to things the same way; it had been so easy to form a friendship with her. Now that I've gotten to know Betsy more and became friends with her, my friendship with both women seemed entirely different from each other.

I thought back to high school and remembered Joyce and Terri, my two best friends. They were different, too. Joyce and I would get together and figure out what outfits to wear on Saturday night for the youth center dance. When we hung out, we always had lots of fun, laughing, and talking about boys. Whatever we did, we had the best time. Sarah's like Joyce.

Then there was Terri. I could always count on her. Even years later, she was there. She was fun-loving, too. At times, we could get into trouble with all her goofy plans, but she was more down to earth. Dependable. When Daniel and I broke up once, Terri was the only friend I wanted to call and she was the first one I called when Daniel gave me my diamond engagement ring. We're still friends, but I'm not sure whatever happened to Joyce.

Betsy is like Terri.

Once, I had said to my mother that I couldn't decide which of my friends was my *best* friend. My mother told me that I didn't have to choose a best friend. "All friends are important and special," she said. Then she reminded me of a song about friendship from the Girl Scouts. The song lyrics sang about old and new friends being like silver and gold and you should keep and value both. Friendships many differ but they are just like silver and gold—both precious.

Yeah, I'm glad Sarah is coming over tonight. Besides, she makes awesome desserts.

* * *

I locked the door to the store at nine o'clock sharp. I had counted the cash drawer around ten after eight because business had been so slow. Nobody came in after that, therefore I only had to lock the money up and turn the lights off.

I realized when I got in the car that I was excited about Sarah's visit. *Yeah, Sarah is just like Joyce,* I thought. *No matter how mad I got at Joyce or how much she messed up, somehow she'd make me forget about it so we could be friends again.*

Still, it was long past my high school years and I wondered if my friendship with Sarah could ever go back to what it had been. I knew now that any sharing from her would be selective. The one sure thing I knew was that I didn't want to share anything with Sarah except laughs, now or in the future.

I'd barely gotten in my front door when the phone rang.

I picked it up, and before I had a chance to say hello, I heard Sarah's voice. "Hi, I wanted to make sure you were home before I headed over. Did everything go okay at the store tonight?"

"Yes, it was pretty quiet."

"I made crème brûlée and a luscious sauce with raspberries to put on top. I made chocolate pudding for Tony and the girls. They'd rather have anything chocolate than a fancy dessert. Tony's fine with me coming over. Since he didn't have to put the girls to bed, he went straight to the den while I was clearing the table. I think he's glad I won't be here to try to get him to visit with me."

She was a runaway train. I knew not to even try to speak.

"He usually works until three or four in the morning. Anyway, I got to read three stories to the girls, *Peter Cottontail,*

Thidwick the Big-Hearted Moose, and *Horton Hears a Who.* They fell asleep during Horton. I'll leave now, okay?"

"Okay, I'm going to change into pajamas while you're on your way," I said. "You don't mind, do you?"

"Oh, no. I'd put on mine if I weren't afraid that some of the neighbors might see me in them on the drive over. It will be like a pajama party, but only one of us will be in pajamas."

About twenty-five minutes later the doorbell rang. I opened it and Sarah entered arms full with bags and talking a continuous streak.

"I got the dessert and I bought three bottles of white wine. I don't know if it is any good, I don't know about wine," she said, passing by me on her way to my kitchen. "I picked them up on the way home today. Oh, yeah, I brought some wine glasses too, just in case you don't have any. We wouldn't want to have to drink wine out of paper cups like in high school. Tony always says you're not supposed to drink and eat sugar together, for some reason; supposedly it'll give you a big hangover or something. Anyway, who cares if we have a hangover? Nobody will know but us. Tony will still be working when I get home and asleep in the morning until right before I leave for work at lunchtime. As if, he'd notice anything about me anyway. I'm your boss at work so I'm giving us permission tonight to par-ty. Right?"

"Right," I yelled back because Sarah was in the kitchen now.

There wasn't any need to follow her. She was a woman on a mission. She hit the kitchen in a flurry of activity, opening cabinets, grabbing plates, and unpacking what she brought. Up until now, I never heard her talk about Tony being inattentive, and now this was the second time today she spoke of it. I wondered if things were starting to go wrong with them. Usually, Sarah spoke about the girls, but rarely about Tony. Maybe I just never noticed before now.

Two hours and one empty wine bottle later, we had listened to some great *golden oldies* music. We had started with Donna Summers then some of the real old stuff like the *Doors, Janis Joplin, The Rolling Stones*, and of course, the *Beatles* and the *Beach Boys*. We drank, laughed and danced to all the greats. We revved up the volume as loud as we could to the rebellious songs of the '60s, singing to *War* and *In the Year 2525*.

Yeah, by then we were pretty well sloshed. When Sarah heard the song, *Ruby*, with the chorus begging, *Ruby don't take your love to town*, Sarah cried as it played.

Somewhere around one o'clock, during Cher's "Gypsies, Tramps and Thieves," Sarah said with a bitterness in her voice, "Yeah, it's always the woman's fault."

Then Sarah looked at me and asked, "Do you think I'm bad? I mean, am I selfish? Tony says I always want everything my way."

Shocked, I sputtered, "No Sarah. You're not selfish. You're always thinking of your girls and Tony. Think about it, tonight you made two desserts because your family likes chocolate."

"I just want to be a good mother and wife. Tony says we had it made before we moved here. I made good money, but I never had time with the girls. They grow up so quickly. I didn't want to miss this time when they're so young. Tony misses the money and doing things like partying with other couples."

"Tony's wrong," I said. "If anything happened and the girls weren't here, there's nothing that can bring this time back. People are important, not money or things."

"Tony doesn't see it that way. Oh, he loves the girls. Don't get me wrong. But he judges a person by how much money they earn. I used to get a paycheck and was important. Now I just work for myself and I'm a mother. He never says anything, but I know he sees me differently now. He still talks to people he used to work with and when he hears of one of the women in the office getting a promotion, boy does he *ever* talk about *her* for weeks."

Then *Go Away Little Girl* by Donnie Osmond started playing and we both began to cry. It probably wasn't the song because we had just opened our third bottle of wine.

Sarah left somewhere after two-thirty, laughing as she got in her car. Maybe I should have made her stay the night and drive home in the morning. However, I was afraid Tony would be angry. I always thought he was so "with it," the perfect husband. I guess like Betsy says, *you never know what goes on behind closed doors.*

Boy, I remember having poker parties when Daniel and I were married. Some of our friends who left our house couldn't even walk a straight line, let alone drive a car safely. We never thought about making them stay or taking the keys away from them. Now in the '80s, there's *Mothers Against Drunk Driving.* Everyone is so aware of things.

When I was pregnant with Lily, doctors were just starting to think that maybe a mother-to-be shouldn't drink. Daniel hovered constantly. He would've had me stay in bed until Lily was born just to play it safe, but even Daniel told me one drink would be okay. Things are different now, a lot different.

I climbed the stairs and poured myself into bed. Morning would be here soon enough. I was glad I had been the one who wore the pajamas for the pajama party. Before surrendering to sleep, I thought, *I'm glad Sarah said I could open the store late tomorrow.*

The Morning After

Sunlight spilled into my bedroom window, waking me. Groggy, I looked at the clock. *Ten o'clock! Is that ten o'clock? I can't believe it.*

I blinked, trying to wake up. I pushed myself up on my elbows, groaned, and then collapsed back down. I definitely needed more time to get my wits about me before getting out of bed.

Good thing Sarah said I didn't have to worry about opening on time. If I'm lucky, I'll get there before she does at noon. Now I know the cure for insomnia. Prescription: finish three bottles of wine.

As I started to get up again, the phone rang. "Whoa, not so loud," I said, stumbling to the phone before it rang again. *Who could be calling me now?*

I got to the phone before it rang the third most-annoying loud ring. "Hello!"

"Not so loud, Stephanie. It's me, Sarah. Were you awake?"

"Just. I'm glad I'm friends with my boss because I'm going to be late today."

"Yeah, I'm glad I own the store. I don't even care what time we open. Guess Tony was right about eating sweets while drinking, or maybe, this is the way we'd feel after three bottles of wine no matter what, but I feel lousy."

"I'll try to get ready and get to the store within half an hour," I said. "Try is the word to remember here. My head is throbbing. I'm not moving too quickly."

After we hung up, I washed my face, put on a little make-up, and took some aspirin. I threw some clothes on and was out of the house in twenty minutes, and by then the tom-tom drums in my head were starting to ease up.

At the store, as I opened up, all the other shopkeepers came out of their shops wanting to know why the late opening. I had to reassure them, one by one, that nothing bad had happened. I was just late. A little white lie to keep between Sarah and me. The S.O.S. pair was back in action, with a new secret that involved drinking, dancing, and pajama party tales.

After a few customers straggled in, made some purchases, and left, I called Betsy. "Hi. I was wondering if you wouldn't mind if I skipped coming by today. I'm a little tired and would like to go straight home after work."

"No, I don't mind," Betsy said. "We really can't do any more checking about the Brewers here in Havenridge so there wouldn't be any need to come by other than for a visit. However, I can tell you what I've found out about Mabel Brewer's mother. I think you may want to drive over to Milledgeville on your day off next week."

"Milledgeville? Is that the town Sarah goes to pick up merchandise for the store?" I asked.

"Yes, it used to be the capital of Georgia years ago. Back around the eighteen hundreds that is. Georgia joined the Confederate States, becoming known as the "Republic of Georgia" after General Sherman marched through Milledgeville. Most people only remember him going through Atlanta or

Savannah. When the Reconstruction began, the capital was moved to Atlanta."

"Really, I didn't know that. Although, I guess most Southerners do," I said.

"Oh, I'm not so sure most of them do," Betsy replied. "I just always enjoyed reading about history, especially things related to Georgia. Anyway, back then, Milledgeville was very prosperous. Of course, it suffered after the capital became Atlanta. Milledgeville was kind of a symbol of the Old South and Atlanta became the symbol of the New South. I think Mabel's mother lived in Milledgeville, I don't know why or for how long. There's a big hospital there. I don't think we'll find out anything more unless one of us goes over there. Maybe check the hospital records. That could've been where she went when she disappeared from Havenridge."

"Okay, I'll go. I have some other papers I found with some doctors' names on them. It's a good bet she was at the hospital. I'll go next Monday. Thanks, Betsy, I couldn't have found out all these things without your help."

"Well, it helps to have lived here all your life, and being a history buff sometimes comes in handy," Betsy replied. "Call me when you come back."

***

Sarah came in around twelve-thirty, apologizing for not bringing lunch. She said she still didn't feel so hot. We both agreed next time we would limit ourselves to no more than two bottles of wine, at the most.

I hurried home to check out some of the entries in Cain's journal and clean up the house. Steve would be back tomorrow.

He was stopping here on his way back from his photoshoot. Two visits in one week. Somehow, I felt that I wasn't as much of an influence on his plans for a return trip as a pretty blond lady with a ponytail that lived up on the hill.

Milledgeville

THE FOLLOWING WEEK:
My drive to Milledgeville took about forty-five minutes, maybe a little longer. I don't know if the abbreviated history lesson Betsy gave me had anything to do with my impression, nevertheless, the town did have an Old South air about it. There was a little bit of a city bustling though, probably because of the college in the middle of town that added busy students to the mix of people.

I decided to park my car and walk around to get a feel for the town before asking any questions. I didn't sense the same underlying unwelcome feeling the people of Havenridge gave me from the people on the street in Milledgeville. Even though this town was part of the Deep South, and fairly small, it still radiated more of a big-city attitude of *it's none of our business* air about it. There was a variety of businesses and the assortment of people abundant. I could see why Sarah liked to come here to check out new trends for the store.

My plan was to go into one of the stores and strike up a conversation with a sales clerk. I had hoped to get some info about the hospital Betsy said was here. One thing I had observed from Betsy was that you got a lot more out of people by making statements than asking questions. After watching Betsy in action, I had learned that people were more eager to talk to you if you acted as if you already knew everything and didn't need their help. It influences them to reveal that they know more than you do.

I walked across Wayne Street and turned on Hancock. The brick-paved intersection had a turnabout and in the middle of the circle, there was a bronze statue. Three benches lined the statue and seemed to beckon me. It had been a long drive and I figured there was no harm stopping to rest before visiting the stores.

I crossed the street and chose a seat next to an elderly man. I turned to admire the beautiful statue of a winged angel with his arm raised. The folds sculpted in the clothing, and other intricate details were masterfully done.

"It's just beautiful," I remarked to the man.

"Yes, it was custom-made for the town. We refer to it as the *Angel of Milledgeville.*

I noticed several stems of fresh roses at the base. "Why are there roses?" I asked, pointing to them. "Is it a memorial?"

He shook his head, "College kids! They have claimed the statue as their own, turned it into a tradition to pledge their love for one another. Couples come here, not to admire the statute, but to place a rose at the feet of the angel as a sign that they are sweethearts. City workers have to pick up the dead roses every couple of days."

"Oh."

I was about to say it sounded like a nice tradition when I looked up and saw Sarah heading toward us. My hand shot up automatically to wave, and then I stopped, pulling my hand down fast. The blinding sun momentarily blocked my vision, but now the view of her was crystal clear. There was no mistake, it was Sarah, but the man's hand she was holding didn't belong to Tony.

They were coming straight toward me. Eyes locked in each other's gaze, laughing and snuggling close. The man was much taller than Tony, with wavy, light brown hair. He looked at Sarah with absolute attention, as if the world didn't exist beyond her. Sarah's eyes sparkled with a life that I'd never seen before, not even when she spoke about the girls. That's when my eyes fell upon the single red rose in the man's hand.

My stomach sank and I felt a rush of panic. Instantly, I wished I were invisible. "It was nice talking to you," I said, abruptly cutting off what the man was saying. "I have to go now."

I popped up and cupped my hand over my eyes, hoping to conceal my face, spinning around to look for an escape. *I can't have her see me. It would be awful for her.*

In front of me, across the street, was a store. I bolted toward it. As I got to the store door, I dared to glance back. Sarah and the man were facing each other with the rose between them. Sarah smiled broadly, as he placed the rose at the base of the statue.

Opening the store door without any thought, I rocketed through the entrance. The bell over the door crashed back and forth, making the loudest clanging sound I'd ever heard in my life. Customers' heads whipped around and stared at me with puzzled looks on their faces.

I looked at them, "Oh, I tripped. Sorry. I'm always making grand entrances." Then I gave a weak little laugh.

It was a lame excuse. However, the only one I could come up with instantly. It worked because everyone went back to shopping. I turned to the window to catch Sarah and her strong, rugged man walking down the block, now arm in arm. They stopped at the corner, passionately kissed, and then continued down the street like two lovers oblivious to the world around them.

It all made sense. All the secrecy, having Betsy come in on my day off. An affair! *How could I have been so naïve?* When Sarah talked about herself, she always created an ideal family picture, but now that I thought about it. She had always spoken either in the past tense, or the abstract. I remembered her telling me about moving to Havenridge. She had said, "We thought it would be perfect." *Would—past tense, like she knew better now.*

And the night of our pajama party, her melancholy, her words replayed in my head. "I know Tony *loves* the children." It sounded like a statement as if it was a consolation prize for him not loving her. She sounded so sad, so unemotional when she spoke about Tony going into his office to work right after dinner. I should've recognized the familiar sound of loneliness. Sarah sure didn't look lonely just a minute ago. I wondered who had been lonely first, her or Tony.

Daniel went out of town regularly, leaving me alone most of my married life. His work always demanded his time, and there were the lecture commitments that took him all over the country. I remember being so lonesome, yearning for adult company. But I didn't cheat on my husband!

Then I recalled Sarah's statement about Tony going on and on about the woman who was promoted at his old office. Yet, he never acknowledged Sarah's hard work. I realized that there are ways to quit a marriage without physically leaving. *I need to leave it alone and forget what I saw. Betsy was right; you never know what goes on behind closed doors.*

My reason for coming to Milledgeville was to find out something about the Brewer family. I needed to get on with it. I walked over to the sales clerk in a corner of the store who was busy putting plants in macramé holders on a display pole.

"Hello, I need some help."

"Yes, ma'am," she said.

"I was wondering, do you live here in Milledgeville?"

She smiled and answered, "Yes."

She was young and too polite to comment that my question was stupid because where else would she live. Thinking I had picked the wrong person to approach since she was young and obviously healthy, however, I had no option but to plow right ahead.

She waited.

"I live over in Havenridge," I said. "I have a friend who told me her great-grandmother at one time was a patient at a hospital over here. I guess I'm being nosey, but, do you know anything about the hospital?"

My brother's words came into my head then. He always said people don't know when to stop talking and wait. Steve had worked at the newspaper for a while and used to go out with one of the crime reporters. They were on assignment, following a bank robbery in the neighborhood of one of the suspects. A search warrant had been presented, and family and neighbors of the suspect stood on the sidewalk, watching as police came out of the house with bags of would-be evidence. The angry crowd wasn't talking to reporters or police. Steve and the reporter stood next to the elderly mother of the suspect, wearing their press badges.

"Man, the police decided he's involved," the reporter had said in protest. "They don't want to listen to any of the people who knew him. They've made up their minds that he's guilty, already."

Then he shut his mouth and never asked the first question. Turned out, the reporter got an exclusive interview with the mother that day. Just by making a statement and shutting up.

She asked him to interview her and write about what she thought. Steve ran the camera.

So, I followed the example and I stood in front of the girl and kept my mouth shut. It was hard, but I did it, and it worked. The young girl, Candy was her name, loved to talk. I guess I underestimated how much young people can know about things in a town.

"All the kids know about the hospital," Candy said with a long, southern drawl. "Our parents have stories. Used to be when children misbehaved, the adults would threaten them that they'd be sent to the asylum. Said that's where bad children were locked up. Can you imagine that?"

I shook my head in disbelief and waited.

"That's what they called it back then, an insane asylum," Candy continued, without missing a beat. "Over the years, the hospital had lots of names. State Asylum for the Insane and Georgia State Sanitarium were some, now it's called Central State Hospital. My friend's mother had a nervous breakdown and she's at the hospital. Although, the place looks pretty now with big, open grassy areas and huge shade trees around. Not like before. I understand it used to be an awful place. Years back. It was like that everywhere then. People not crazy, who had epilepsy, were locked up, back then. Even a husband could have the doctor commit his wife by just saying she had a problem. How awful would that be? To be locked up because you made your husband angry?"

"It would be pretty awful," I said. I hoped by agreeing and showing an interest, it would keep her talking.

"Yes. It was awful. But that was a long time ago. My other friends and me don't talk about those stories with Holly; she's the one whose mom is there."

Candy hung the last plant on the display pole, gathered up the packing paper, and threw it in the empty box. She picked the box up and turned to me.

"I'd better go now. The hospital is not far from here. You probably could get more information from the office staff. It was real nice talking to you, and I don't think you're nosy. Good luck."

Wow, an insane asylum, I thought. Now the secrecy makes sense, if Cain had his wife committed. Wonder if she was insane or she just made him mad at her.

Hanna Brewer's letters sounded crazy, at least some of them. Others only sounded sad. If she'd been locked away and not sick, that would certainly make anyone become paranoid and really go a little crazy. I left the store where Candy worked and nosed around in a few different stores. I got the location and directions to the hospital from a clerk where I bought some kitchen towels.

The day was full. I spent a good four hours in Milledgeville; however, I never ran into Sarah again. Of course, I kept an eagle eye out for her and her mystery man. I didn't want any more surprises. I stopped by the hospital before leaving for Havenridge.

Driving home, I thought about everything I had learned and could hardly wait to tell Betsy about what I'd found out, except for the part about seeing Sarah and Mr. Handsome.

I knew now I wanted to share everything with Betsy that I had found in old man Brewer's secret space. I don't know why I kept some of the things to myself. I hope Betsy will understand about me not trusting her. Although it wasn't truly about not trusting her, it was just that my past had conditioned me not to trust anyone.

Secrets Revealed

I was exhausted by the time I got home and collapsed into bed. My fatigue was a good kind. It came from hard investigative work. Steve used to talk about the rush of adrenaline he observed from the reporters. They lived on coffee, worked weird hours, and had the stress of daily deadlines, all for a chance to get that next great story before someone else did. The concept was so foreign to me. Steve had said one reporter compared it to riding a bucking bronco and never knowing when you would get thrown out of the competition. I was beginning to understand that crazy rush that came with unraveling a hidden story.

I felt determined more than ever to dig into the mysteries of the Brewers. I wondered about how different Mabel's life would've been in another time, without society's strict rules.

Steve's insight that he brought to his photography, searching for form and balance, said he used it with everything in life. This skill gave him a unique understanding of people. How people lived and why they did certain things. Steve knew how to dig and go beneath the surface. He could cut through a mystery and get to the heart of why people reacted the way they did as if he had a compass that led to their souls. I hoped to learn how to read people like Steve does.

His words flashed into my mind. "Everything is perspective, Steph. Life doesn't happen haphazardly. We all have choices. There's a yin and yang to life."

Cain Brewer must have had his reasons for why he lived the way he did and why he dominated his daughter's life.

"Life's all around us, Steph,' Steve would say. It's like a flowing river, taking you where you're supposed to be—if you allow it."

I felt it now, the force of the river. I'd been stuck in time with Lily. I was afraid to move on—didn't want to, like Mabel had been stuck. The river of life is *energy*. Mabel, Cain, and Hanna have dislodged my trapped spirit.

I'm moving again. I feel alive. Awakened.

***

I arrived at work ten minutes early. I dusted everything in the store in a whirlwind of energy and swept the front sidewalk, all before eleven-thirty. Then, with nothing to do, I walked outside and visited with the shopkeepers next door. I reassured them that everything was fine and normal, easing their concerns about my early arrival this morning. Early or late, they worried.

I even enjoyed Miss Gladys's visit. She stopped in on her way to the church office. Of course, she was properly dressed, complete with pearls and white gloves, even though the temperature was already eighty-nine degrees. She explained she had to get the programs typed and printed for this week's service. Little Rachael Harrison was going to sing two solos this Sunday, and she wanted to invite me.

"Rachael has an extraordinary voice. A true gift from God," Gladys said. I thought that perhaps I would go. I needed to show a desire to be part of the community.

Sarah came in at one forty-five. At first, I couldn't look her in the eye. I kept thinking about her and the other man in her life. Then I thought of Betsy. Betsy took everyone at face value and Sarah's value was good. She had a giving heart. I only wished that Sarah would credit herself as much as she credited everyone else. She was always in awe of everyone. Sarah used to say she thought that most people had the ability to achieve anything. She'd said, more than once, that she wished she could be like everyone else and know exactly the right things to do.

Sarah was unusually bubbly when she came into the store. She wore a new summery top with white leggings underneath and white flats. The blouse was mauve with little tan geometric shapes.

When I told her how great she looked, she said, "Thanks, it makes me feel pretty. Someone I know told me that it makes my green eyes stand out." She paused. "I don't think Tony remembers what color my eyes are, let alone notice a new outfit."

I guess I know who noticed her eyes. Mr. Handsome, no doubt. Come to think of it, Sarah was always upbeat the day after my day off. It was good to see Sarah happy, not that I condoned an affair. We all have our little secrets. Maybe that's part of life. No matter how much you think you know someone, there's always something, either in their past or happening now, that you don't know about them. People wear all kinds of masks. Except for Betsy. She was an open book.

Sieving through Papers

It was five minutes before eight when I finished washing the dishes and heard Betsy's knock at the front door. We settled down at the dining room table with some iced tea, ready to tackle the stacks of papers I'd organized. I told Betsy about little Candy in Milledgeville. Then we dug into Cain's journal. The entries were starting to make more sense now. There were more mentions of Dr. Greenfield. A blurry picture of a family's past was coming into focus.

"Betsy, I spoke to a head nurse at the hospital. She said there was a Dr. Greenfield in charge, back in the early years. She took me to an area that displayed portraits of past administrators of the hospital and I saw one of Dr. Greenfield, and also, a Dr. Copper. The nurse, Cora, was very helpful. She told me records dated as far back as we needed aren't kept at the hospital. They had been packed in boxes and sent to storage in Atlanta. We're going to have to fill out some forms to request copies of the records from there. It'll probably take a little bit of time."

We put Cain's journal aside and tackled Hanna and Cain's letters. After a bit of time, Betsy suggested, "Why don't we read and organize the letters in chronological order. That way we can connect them to the entries in the journal of the same time frame."

This took hours, but it enabled us to start conquering a puzzle more than one hundred years old. It was late and Betsy and I agreed we couldn't read anymore. We were both starting to see double. As we rested for a minute, our eyes scanned the piles before us. Then Betsy's eyes stopped at a specific stack of envelopes and she reached for them.

"Stephanie, these are addressed to Mabel but they've never been opened. If these were hidden in the crawl space that means she must not have known they existed. Maybe they're from her mystery lover, the one Clarence told us about, the drifter and boyfriend old man Brewer ran off."

"Clarence told us Mabel's father was controlling. I bet you're right," I said. "If she never knew about them, then she died thinking her lover abandoned her. How sad for her. How could a father do that to his daughter?"

"It was a different era," Betsy said. "Back then, being a good father meant making choices for his family, and for whatever reason, Cain thought Mabel's drifter wasn't good for her. We need to read these letters the next time we get together. It's too late tonight."

"Betsy, thank you so much. You know how to deal with disconnected pieces of information and assemble everything so it makes sense. You make everything seem so simple."

"It's not that hard," she said. "You just have to step into the detective's shoes by thinking in the attitudes of that generation."

"You've been a good friend to me," I said. "I know I can always count on you."

I felt the quietness of the evening coming to an end. This was a good time to tell Betsy about my daughter, Lily. All evening, Betsy was so intuitive and compassionate to the emotions of Hanna and Cain, people she didn't even know.

There was so much tenderness in Betsy's soul. I wanted her to know everything about me.

"I don't feel I deserve your support," I said.

"Deserve my support? Why would you say such a thing, Stephanie?"

"You don't understand. I haven't been completely truthful with you. You've been so open and caring. I'm not the person you think I am."

"Stephanie, no one ever truly knows someone. There are things deep inside, private things that people keep to themselves. You act like you killed someone," Betsy said.

I didn't know if I had the courage to tell Betsy about Lily now. Betsy had shown respect for me and I didn't want to give that up. If she knew the truth, no telling how she would feel about me.

"Could you still be friends with a killer?"

"How can I answer that?" Betsy shook her head as if I were being silly. "I don't know any killers." She stood and picked our glasses up, clearing the table.

"But you do know a killer."

Betsy froze and turned to me.

"My daughter is dead," I said. "She died because of me. I didn't mean for her to die, but she did. Just the same as if I had taken a gun to her head and pulled the trigger."

Betsy placed the glasses on the table and sat down.

Her opinion of me mattered. It had been a little more than a year since I had met Betsy and Joe. I had grown to admire them. Betsy had a pure love of her fellow man. To accept such complete trust from her without being honest, keeping my secret from her was nothing more than a malicious lie.

"The police brought me in for questioning after my daughter, Lily, died. They said that neglect caused her death. That I waited too long to take her to the hospital."

The look on Betsy's face had changed. *Was it confusion or discomfort?* Her pure heart probably couldn't comprehend knowing anyone capable of any kind of wrongdoing, least of all being responsible for a child's death.

"All you know about me is what I've told you," I said. I had to explain. I could no longer keep up the charade. "The truth is my little girl died and it's *my* fault." It was the first time I had said it out loud. *It's my fault. Lily is dead because of me.*

My body started to shake and tears streamed down my face. I had thought that I couldn't cry anymore, that I had dried up long ago. Sobbing, I didn't know if my tears were because of Lily, or because I had betrayed Betsy.

"Stephanie, how could you think it was your fault?" Betsy's soft voice seemed to be far away, like when you're coming out of a deep sleep and waking up.

"You had no way of knowing she would have a reaction to the medicine. You were caring for her, trying to help her get well," Betsy words flowed over me.

"No. You don't understand. I was the wife of a doctor. Allergic drug reactions being potentially fatal, breathing airways closing off; these were things I knew about. If I had checked on her when I heard her breathing strangely, I might have gotten her to the hospital before it was too late." Then Betsy's words penetrated my mind. Through my sobs, I gulped for air and I tried to regain control of my body. I drew in a breath . . . "What did you say?"

"I said it wasn't your fault. You can't blame yourself."

"You know about Lily?"

"Yes. When you moved here, I knew I'd seen you before, but I couldn't place where. It was funny how it came back to me. The day we went to the courthouse together to look up some information on the Brewers. You said that you wondered why courthouses always had steps leading up to them. Commenting that even in Florida, one of the flattest states in America, there were steps leading up to the courthouse."

"I do remember saying that to you. That day was sunny like the day Daniel and I walked out of the Orlando courthouse. The grand jury decided there was no probable cause to charge me. However, I was still guilty in the eyes of the news. Leaving the courthouse, the reporters swarmed us on the steps, snapping pictures and making horrible accusations."

"That picture of you and your husband on the courthouse steps is how I made the connection. Your hair was lighter and the first name in the papers was different, but there was no doubt it was you."

I wiped my eyes and said, "Most of the time the newspaper referred to me as Rebecca Oliver. Stephanie is my middle name. That was what I used to go by, except for signing legal papers. I changed my name legally before moving to Havenridge."

"It must have been awful being brought in for questioning about your daughter's death only days before her funeral," Betsy said.

"The police didn't believe Lily's death was an accident. They thought I had been overburdened by raising my daughter with my husband away so often. After I gave her the medicine, Lily had trouble breathing. The police thought I watched her struggling to breathe and waited but panicked, and then raced her to the hospital. Shortly after we got to the hospital, she died."

Betsy slammed the table. "That's just absurd! Your husband called in the medicine. He didn't know she would have a reaction and *he's* the doctor. No mother would watch her child struggling to breathe."

Betsy was mad, but not at me.

"But, but I didn't check on her. The police said I was either incredibly stupid or negligible. Most of my friends agreed that I should have checked on her earlier."

"Well then, you had stupid friends," Betsy said firmly.

I sat stunned. She knew who I was and never questioned that I had been a good mother. When I came to Havenridge, I thought no one would know me or that I had been accused of murdering my daughter.

Betsy smoothed out the tablecloth, apparently taking a moment to collect her thoughts. Then she spoke, "Even though I followed the story I wouldn't have connected you if it hadn't been for that photograph. That picture was plastered all over the papers, even in our little local one. I'd been working in the sheriff's department at the time and all my co-workers were following the story."

"You never said anything to me," I said, "or anyone else?"

"Of course not. I realized it hadn't come to anyone's attention other than mine. Probably because of the name. You never mentioned having had a daughter, so I figured you didn't want people here to know. So I kept it to myself."

"Do you think anyone else in town made the connection?" I asked.

"No. If anyone did, everyone would be talking about it." Betsy turned to me, "Stephanie, why would you blame yourself? A mother can't protect her child from everything."

"You can't understand, Betsy. You're not a mother. Even if I didn't hear her gasping for air, I should've sensed it. I didn't keep her safe. I may not be guilty of a crime in the eyes of the law, but a mother shouldn't live after her child dies."

"Don't say such things! It is not for you to judge others. How dare you?"

"Betsy, I'm not talking about other people, just me."

"To speak with so little respect for life is speaking against God. I won't listen to it," Betsy said tersely. "You're not the only one who has lost a child."

I couldn't believe what I was hearing. "Betsy, you lost a child?"

She was almost in tears now. I realized I'd always sensed her deep loneliness, never realizing we shared a grief of losing a child.

As Betsy spoke about her past, I became aware that I knew very little about her life. I never thought to ask her about her yesterdays. Life's road traveled, is a very intricate part of who we are and how we live. Our yesterdays are so very important. I listened to Betsy's recalling of another time. Her journey.

Betsy began, "Joe and I had a beautiful little girl named Jennifer. She was seven, happy, and healthy. Then there was an accident, and she was gone.

No chance for doctors to give her medicine to try to help her."

If I had a fatal car accident, I would never be able to forgive myself. Betsy somehow had moved forward with life.

"How do you keep from blaming yourself?" I asked. "Even with Joe's love and support, how can you be happy after losing your daughter?" I asked. "For me, I tried, but I still can't let go of the guilt."

"There's no blame to give," Betsy said.

My heart ached for her. Maybe that's what had drawn us together from the start, an intuitive sense of another mother's tragedy.

Betsy took a deep breath and let it out. "Joe was driving."

My throat tightened. I understood Daniel not being able to forgive me. I couldn't imagine being in his position and having to give forgiveness. Betsy and Joe are so loving toward each other. *How could Betsy still love him, if he was the one who was responsible?*

Minutes passed in silence. I tried to take in what I had just heard.

Betsy spoke again. "People say that when a tragedy occurs, only one of two things happens. It will break a couple apart, or bring them closer together. I guess some couples are so lost in the grief; it is as if they're in a dark hole, and all they can do is grope for a way out. For Joe and me, the only way out of the darkness was to hang on to each other. Losing Jenny was too unbearable to go through without one another. I can't think of life without Joe. Our bond is how we filled the hollow space left by our little girl."

Betsy's description of the hollow that grief puts you into was so clear. Daniel and I were lost in the darkness. For us, we needed to take different paths out.

She continued, "Joe was hurt *bad* from the accident. The doctors thought he might die. He must've sensed our daughter was gone, and perhaps that's why he wasn't fighting to live. He was in a coma. A nurse came to me and asked me to talk to Joe. She thought my voice might help give him the will to fight death. When they rolled my bed into his room and I saw him, I cried. I told him I needed him, that without him I would be lost forever."

"Betsy, I'm so sorry. Maybe you and Joe will have other children. I know people used to tell me that and I wanted to kill them for saying it. But you have each other. For me, my marriage couldn't survive. You and Joe's love for each other is so strong. You both have so much to give to a child. You need to be parents."

"No," Betsy shook her head. "Once the ambulance got to the hospital, I was rushed into surgery. My injuries were too severe. I can't have any more children. Stephanie, life is a gift. You can't turn your back on it. You see, not only is it against God to stop living and blame yourself, it doesn't honor the life you had with Lily. Just like it wouldn't honor my little Jenny if Joe had given up."

My brother had urged me to move on, to resume my life, and be happy. Still, I couldn't snap out of my grief. Maybe an angel was nudging Betsy tonight to share her heartache with me. Nevertheless, I was ready to listen, now. I could start living again without feeling I needed to be punished for it.

We sat for a long time in silence. When Betsy left, she said she hoped I'd start honoring Lily. I promised her I would. Yet, I needed to keep Lily private between her and me. It wasn't really a secret anymore, it was just my way to protect the happy memories of Lily. I didn't want people to focus on her death when they saw me.

I said that I hoped we would talk again about our daughters. I wanted Betsy to *know* my Lily. Know things about her. Like how she loved kittens, her favorite color was yellow, and she loved butterflies. She hated peanut butter and jelly sandwiches, and how swinging high scared her. Sharing these things with Betsy would make me happy.

Betsy said she looked forward to hearing the happy things about Lily.

"I think our daughters would've been good friends if they had met before they died," I said. "I bet they are friends and play together now."

Betsy gasped, putting her hand to her mouth. After a second, she said, "That was the one thing I've never been able to get past. I was afraid Jenny would be lonely after being snatched away from her earthly friends. Little girls need to have friends their age, especially if they have to leave their daddy and mommy behind," Betsy smiled and then said, "I'm sure that is why we met."

Changing Tides

During the next few weeks, the task of calling Milledgeville hospital on the phone to track information down resulted in multiple dead ends. After more calls than I want to remember, each peppered with frustration, I finally reached the right department and the person to talk to about patient information. However, that's when the real battle started.

The voice on the other end of the line asked, "What did you say your name was," in a tone that made me feel as if a hundred-watt light bulb shone directly in my face. "And why do you need these records? Are you related in any way to the patient you're inquiring about?"

I explained that I was trying to track down information on a distant relative for an elderly friend who was too frail to fill out the paperwork herself. My friend asked for my help and suggested that I write a book about the hospital's history. It wasn't really a lie. Mabel Brewer and her family were guiding me, indirectly. I hoped the ego effect would kick in as Betsy and I had seen in Clarence, and she would feel important if she could help. I was wrong. Importance wasn't what she needed. She already had power and knew it.

"Well, madam, such records cannot be released to just anyone," the obstinate voice said from the other end of the line. "You need to look somewhere else."

"But I'll fill out the proper forms," I argued with mounting impatience. "You'll have information about who I am. I'll pay for any copies made."

"There are confidential papers involved. You're not a family member."

"I just. . . need you . . . to send . . . the . . . request forms," I said through clenched teeth. "You don't have to be the one to approve them."

"I'm not head of the department. Of course, I wouldn't be the one to approve the request."

The woman wouldn't budge. Lifting possible blame from her shoulders didn't sway her at all.

"Now I have work to do, madam. Goodbye."

I heard a click then the dial tone buzzed in my ear. I slammed the phone down, exasperated. I didn't know if I was going to scream or cry. I had hit a brick wall.

I needed to call Betsy, she might know what to do. After I vented my anger, I asked her if she thought she could get past this female Attila the Hun.

"We may not have access to the patients' medical records," Betsy said. "But it's a state hospital and records of patient admissions should be public record. Let me see what I can find out. I have a friend at the Sheriff's office who might have an answer for us."

The undertaking had been bigger than I'd anticipated and it took months. Bureaucracy moves at a sluggish pace. I don't know how Betsy did it, but by mid-October, a big brown envelope arrived in the mail from Atlanta with a list of patient names.

During those months of waiting and afterward, Steve came for regular visits. However, within a few weeks of his first few visits to my house, he changed his accommodations to Leanne's house. The original excuse was, and these are his words precisely, "Steph, I'm going to be getting in late and I don't want to wake you, not now that you're sleeping well."

He thought that it would be easier on me if he'd stayed with Leanne' and that they'd come over the next day after I got home from work. Although it might have been autumn, love seemed to be blossoming as if it were springtime.

I was glad for Steve. He seemed happier than I'd ever seen him. He took on work differently, more systematic. He thought through every job offer, weighing out the potential of each photoshoot against another, and how it would affect his career and professional reputation.

One night, he even spoke about investing in land.

"I need to own something of value," he said, "that I can leave my children, whenever I have kids." Steve had never spoken like that before.

Everything and everyone in my life had a happier, lighter feel. I even decided to go to Gladys' church for a few visits, and yes, little Rachael's voice was amazing. Betsy, Sarah, and I had regular "girls only" dinner nights at my house. I usually made the salad and appetizers. Sarah insisted on bringing the entrée every time because she said it would give her a chance to try some new recipes out since Tony preferred plain meat and potatoes. Betsy usually brought the dessert.

Sometime between Thanksgiving and the first week of December, Sarah's mood darkened. When I asked if something was wrong, she vaguely replied, "Tony's a little grouchy lately. He's not acting normal. He's constantly asking me where I'm going all the time. He never cared before, and I don't think he really cares now. It's more like he's mad at me for the time I spend at the store or when I have to run errands for work."

She would often finish by saying, "He hasn't been easy to live with. I'm getting tired of making excuses to myself for the mean things he says to me."

Things had changed so much for me this first year in Havenridge. I was happy. I had good friends, and maybe sometime in the future, I would become a sister-in-law. I looked forward to waking up to every new day. However, I sensed a change in Sarah's life, too. I feared she was moving in a much different direction than the happy one I had found.

Connecting the Dots

Betsy and I were burning the midnight oil. We had numbered, dated, and organized every letter. Now that we actually had records of patients at Milledgeville, we had proof that Mabel's mother, Hanna, had been a patient. Cain had committed her two times.

With Betsy's attention to details and her keen memory for dates, she pieced the information together. I was reading one of Hanna's disjointed letters to Cain when Betsy stopped and looked up at me.

"Stephanie, these records show Hanna died at the hospital." She started lifting up papers, looking underneath them, searching for something. "Where's the Brewers' Bible?"

I moved a letter I'd just finished reading that I had placed down and answered, "I've got it here."

"Good, look up the date of Hanna's death. I want to see how old she was when she died," Betsy said.

It was amazing how much information could be found in the family charts in that Bible. I found Hanna's name and I read aloud. "Birth 1864, death 1907."

"I remember one of Cain's entries said he married Hanna when she was sixteen. Stephanie, look for the marriage date."

"Okay. Here it is. Cain Syrus Brewer married Hanna Catherine Crowley, 1881."

"And what's Mabel's birth date?"

I scanned the family chart, "1883."

"The hospital records from Atlanta showed Hanna listed as a patient once in eighteen eighty-one and the second time in eighteen eighty-five. Mabel was only three years old," Betsy said. "When Hanna was committed the second time. Hanna stayed there until her death. Mabel probably didn't have any memories of her mother—wait a minute. I think . . ." Betsy shuffled through the papers on the table. "Here it is. The list of patients. There was an entry, I think," Betsy said as she ran her finger down the list, "yes, I've got it."

"What is it?"

"We were looking only in the years around eighteen eighty-one, eighty-two, or close to that time, but . . . I knew I saw it farther down on the list. There's a Crowley listed in eighteen forty-three. A Josephine Crowley. Do you see a Josephine in the Bible?"

I looked through the list of names, "Yes. Josephine was Mabel's grandmother." A thought made me shudder. "Betsy," I asked. "Can mental illnesses be inherited?"

"Some kinds."

"That's why Cain kept a close rein on his daughter. He was watching Mabel growing up, waiting all those years for Mabel to go crazy like her mother and grandmother," I said. "How sad. With the weight of that kind of fate hanging over his head . . . I wonder how he kept from going crazy himself. No wonder he was so hateful."

The patient list we obtained from Atlanta had columns alongside the names. The headings above the columns were "released," "deceased," "occupation," "hometown" and "diagnosis." If the patient was deceased, the date appeared, if released only "cured" was entered. We found out that if a patient escaped, the entry was still marked "cured." Another curious entry was underneath the column marked diagnosis. There were only three marked choices; they were "insane", "idiotic", or "epileptic".

Our research revealed that if a person didn't conduct himself or herself properly as society thought they should act, then that was sufficient reason for their family to institutionalize them. It was this type of judgment call from family or doctors which opened possibilities of abuse. Often an angry husband of a disobedient wife was the sole reason for her commitment. Which was what the young salesgirl in Milledgeville had said. Furthermore, at one time, people sentenced for crimes were put into the asylums because there was nowhere else to put them when the prisons were full.

Hanna's random delusional writings made it apparent she'd lost touch with reality. Some of her letters laid claim to lengthy conversations with birds outside her window or a small mouse that would sneak under her door and speak to her. Hanna often claimed she talked to people who would come and go by walking through solid walls to escape notice. Whether Hanna's hallucinations were at the crux of why Cain committed her, or if being locked away caused them, we couldn't know.

It felt eerie going through the records. The grief bestowed on the Brewer family hung heavily in the air. It gave me cold chills to think that both mother and grandmother had been committed. Locked away with no hope for a cure. Neither, Hanna or Josephine's name had a release date. Josephine was institutionalized for more than twenty years. Records indicated both stayed there until they left in a coffin. Cain took care of Josephine secretly, not letting Hanna know her mother was still alive.

Betsy listened, while I read aloud Cain's entry in his journal.

Eighteen Eighty-Five, Springtime

    The doctors have told me to send Hanna to Milledgeville for Dr. Cooper to treat her nervous condition. I have told Dr. Cooper about a promise I made to Hanna's father, Reverend Crowley. I pledged I would keep the Reverend's secret and continue to take care of his wife, Josephine, once he passed on, as he had done for years. Josephine lives at the hospital in Milledgeville. Hanna still doesn't know about her mother's continued existence. I've kept the confidence Revenant Crowley bestowed on me.

    I explained to Dr. Cooper at our meeting on Wednesday that Hanna was a baby when Josephine went mad. Hanna's father brought her up believing her mother died giving birth to her. I cannot fault her father for this since his intention was to protect my dear Hanna. My fear now is Hanna will meet her mother while staying at the same hospital and find out she is still alive.

    Dr. Cooper reassured me that Hanna would be kept from the area where her mother is, but I am still haunted by the possibility of their reunion.

    I must send Hanna for treatment. Dr. Cooper is my only hope. I try not to give in to trepidation that the sickness is passed on from mother to daughter. If this is so, recovery for Hanna is doomed and the same fate awaits our precious Mabel.

    I worry I may die in my sleep from a broken heart. This is why I keep my journal. A record for whoever takes my beautiful Mabel into their home when I am gone. Maybe the sickness will skip over, passing Mabel. If that happens, she must have no

*children to inherit the bad blood and cast this perpetual torment
onto her heirs. Only then will our family's curse end.*

"Betsy, this is why Cain wouldn't let Mabel have a beau.
This puts a new light on why a father would, as Clarence's father
said, *want his daughter to be an old maid.* Cain was trying to
protect his daughter the only way he knew how. The upsetting
thing is that nothing was wrong with Mabel. Her happiness was
sacrificed, and for what? What a waste."

"Stephanie, remember the unopened letters addressed to
Mabel? We put them away when we started all the calls and
paperwork requesting the hospital records. We need to open
those letters."

"You're right."

We were so focused on the hospital records that I had
forgotten all about the letters. Once I found the box in the piles
of items gathered together for later, I put it on the table in front
of us. Every member of the Brewer family made up a slice of the
whole picture. What we failed to do was to examine all the
pieces of the puzzle. Mental illness, the doctors, and the
hospital, all shaped and influenced Cain. What he believed, and
did, affected Hanna and Mabel's life.

There were mountains of information that formed building
blocks that completed the landscape of the Brewers' family
history, except for Mabel. A major piece was missing in Mabel's
profile, the love of her life—a lost lover. Her story was told by
gossip traveling from generation-to-generation like wildfire.
Gossip or truth, the story ended with sadness and the abrupt
disappearance of Mabel's lover, a man she never got over losing.

"I bet the unopened letters were from Mabel's drifter
lover," I said. We dug through the contents of the box.

Betsy found the bundle of unopened letters. "Here they are," she said. She untied the string, pulled the top letter out, and ripped it open.

She examined the letter, thumbing through three pages. Reaching the last page, her eyes fell to the bottom.

"Oh no. That's why she moved here and wanted to look into the Brewer history," Betsy said in an almost inaudible voice.

"Who? Who are you talking about, Betsy? What's the signature?"

"It's Jacob . . . Jacob Thompson, Leanne's uncle, the one who was—a wanderer."

A Love Vow

I woke early and stayed in bed trying to clear my foggy mind. I didn't feel rested because I had tossed and turned most of the night.

Jacob Thompson, I thought. *Leanne's great uncle, the one with the wandering spirit, is Mabel's lost love.*

I thought about an interview with a historical writer that I had read a while ago in a magazine. He said when he would listen to personal accounts of the past that people's memories could become clouded. He had to be very careful to get documentation of public records, whenever possible, to prove the authenticity of what he wrote. He claimed people usually remembered names that sounded similar, or had the same beginning initial; however, they would recall a completely different name than the correct one.

If what I had read was right, then it all fits. Clarence said the drifter's name was something like either John or Jack Tyson.

"John or Jack starts with J. The same initial as Jacob," I muttered.

Why did Cain keep all those letters? What purpose did it serve? Maybe Cain thought they would comfort him after Mabel went insane. They would prove that he was right in keeping the two lovers apart. I threw off the sheets and climbed out of bed. I wanted to re-read the letter that Betsy and I read last night. The one Jacob wrote to Mabel saying he would be back to get her within the month.

Betsy told me that Leanne had come to her when she first moved to Havenridge and asked for help digging through courthouse records for any evidence of her uncle having been in Havenridge. However, there weren't any records. No marriage license, no death certificate, nothing. Since Jacob didn't own any land, all of their searching had hit dead-ends.

My search was bringing things into focus. Only, instead of a puzzle becoming a whole picture, I visualized broken and detached pieces before me. A ruined life of a young woman and a final unknown piece, Jacob Thompson, was causing my hope to deflate. The pieces crumbled before me like a house of cards. Although I had to tell Leanne what we had found, I didn't know how to approach her with my findings. I didn't even know exactly what I had uncovered about her uncle, except that he had been here and he loved Mabel.

I grabbed my robe, put on a pair of slippers, and went downstairs. I figured I would read the letter again. Maybe there was some clue we had missed. I was hoping there was something indicating where Jacob went after he left Havenridge. Even if he mentioned how far he was traveling, that would be a start.

Leanne only knew family gossip, not any real facts about what happened to her uncle. However, she had an old letter from her uncle Jacob that she had shown Betsy. Leanne's uncle wrote declaring that he was going to get married and bring his bride home, but he didn't give her name. Then all correspondence abruptly ended. Relatives mocked any notion that the restless uncle would settle down. They believed he had gotten cold feet. He never stayed in one place long enough to fit into a *normal* life. Jacob had always been the black sheep of the family.

Leanne never believed her uncle would write home about plans to marry and suddenly change his mind. She told Betsy that she thought he wouldn't have made such a life-changing decision and not be rock-sure of it. Especially since her family said he never gave a hoot about molding into what everyone else thought he should be and do in life. So, to reach a decision to marry, he *had* to be very much in love. She was certain something must've gone very wrong to stop him.

Downstairs, I found the letter and sat at the kitchen table to read it again.

> *My Dearest Mabel,*
>
> *It will not be long now and I will have enough money earned to come for you. I promise we will build a good life together. The ache I have had in my heart these months away from you has been almost more than I could bear. I have filled the days working to have the security of a full money pouch.*
>
> *Many families are getting ill here. Some of the men have been stricken with the fever.*
>
> *This misfortune on others looks upon us kindly because I have been allowed to pick up the ill men's portion of work. This grants me more money. Do not worry. I am strong. Although I am so very tired, my weary body is able to keep going with the knowledge that the additional funds will get me back to you more quickly.*
>
> *In a few weeks, I will have saved enough money to come and get you. The extra money I have earned can buy supplies to build a sound home. It will not be as grand as your father's house, but*

it will be filled with love and be a good home to raise our children.

All my life I have been of a free mind without ribbons tying me to my family's home. Now my darling Mabel, the only things that fill my mind are images of you.

I am an honest and honorable man. I have worked all my life and have never taken charity. I pledge to you, my darling that we will not sneak away in the dead of night. I will face your father and tell him of my intentions, but I cannot do this with empty pockets.

I promise to you that I will always provide you with food and a warm and happy home. I will come home to you each night to protect and love you.

I have written my family to tell them we will wed and of my plans to return with my bride. Mabel, be strong, it will not be long before we are together again. We will be husband and wife as we have planned. I will be there before the beginning of next month.

Forever faithful,
Jacob

"What stopped him? Why didn't Jacob come back to Mabel?" I said with a heavy heart as I stared at the love letter.

Leanne was right about her uncle. He would've moved heaven and earth for Mabel.

The letter from Jacob proved Leanne was right when she thought something must have gone wrong . . . very wrong.

Sixteen Marks the Date

I had no doubt now about telling Leanne of the Brewer secrets hidden in the house. However, my heart ached with worry for Leanne's feelings. She had become more than a mere acquaintance. If she wanted me to investigate deeper, I would continue. The history belonged to Leanne as much as to Mabel. My investigation, or snooping as Clarence saw it, had a new link that changed everything. Instead of my sole responsibility to Mabel Brewer, because I owned her homestead, I now felt an obligation to the innocent and young Leanne to solve a family mystery.

It had been nearly four short months since that September day of Steve's unannounced visit but so much had changed. Now when Steve visited I never saw him without Leanne. Sharing Steve with Leanne was all right with me, it felt natural. She was interesting, creative, and genuinely kind. Whenever I was near them, I could feel their love for each other. Not that touchy-feely love of a new relationship that makes others feel intrusive and uncomfortable, but a quiet gentleness that radiated all around them. They reminded me a little bit of Betsy and Joe.

I hadn't realized until now that I thought of Steve and Leanne as one. To tell them together about Jacob was the correct thing to do. I didn't remember Steve telling me he had to travel this week so I picked up the phone and dialed his apartment.

"Hello, this is Steve, how may I help you."

Even the way my brother answered the phone was different. So businesslike. So grown-up.

"Steve, I'm glad you're home. I need to talk to you and Leanne, together. When are you coming to town next?"

"Hi, Steph, I'm glad you called. Leanne has been asking if we've talked. I was supposed to call you last week, but I've been busy trying to arrange my schedule. I'm coming there in a week, on the sixteenth. Leanne wanted to do some Christmas shopping together. She and I need to go over our schedules and discuss some things. We need to talk to you, too. When are you available?"

My brother having a schedule? That's certainly different. Steve always *flew by the seat of his pants,* so to speak. That was one of the reasons he did so well in his field. He'd bid photo layouts all over the country and accepted assignments anywhere at a split-second notice. Making himself available for everyone, anywhere, and anytime his whole career. That's how he made his name known. He cultivated hundreds of business contacts. Still, he demanded perfection in his work, no flying by the seat of his pants there. That's why he had a reputation for being the best in his field. *But working on a schedule?* That blew my mind.

We decided on a day and time. "I want to talk to you both about some things I've discovered in my investigation of the Brewer family. Betsy's been so much help, but before I go any further, I need to know what Leanne thinks."

"Leanne? I'm glad you respect her opinion, but why the urgent tone about talking to her?"

"I have my reasons. What about you? Your request sounds like it has a hidden purpose. Is there something significant you both want to talk to me about?"

"Could be, Steph. But you'll have to wait. Leanne thought you could come over for dinner."

I could just see in my mind standing at Leanne's front door with over-stuffed boxes of letters, journals, and all my Brewer research. Visualizing her puzzled look, her asking about the things in my hands. I'd have to answer right there on the spot without any time to ease my way into the information about her uncle. I wasn't up to that scene.

"Dinner would be wonderful," I replied. "But I've got a lot of things here at the house I want to show you. Would she be insulted if I did the cooking and you both came here?"

"No, she'll understand, Sis. A family doesn't have to worry about insulting each other. See you on the sixteenth. Bye."

"Okay. But Steve, you said family understands? Leanne isn't . . . " Before I could say that she wasn't family, Steve stopped me.

"You know what I mean. Leanne is close, kind of like family. I've to go now. See you on the sixteenth. Bye."

"Yes, see you then. Bye."

I can see this year has changed a lot of things. I guess I'll have to wait and see just how much change is in the plans for the future.

Sweet Anticipation

It was Sunday, only one more day until Steve and Leanne's visit. I was so excited. I left the house in plenty of time to get to the store and not be late. Sarah and I pulled into the parking lot together. We were both working full days from now until Christmas, except for taking our usual days off. However, Sarah said she probably would come in a few hours even on her days off.

After our hellos, we got the money drawer out of the safe, turned the open sign over, and started to unpack some Christmas merchandise. We didn't expect our first customer until after church let out. Therefore, by opening early we could get a jump on merchandising for the holiday business. We had just finished unpacking a box of reindeer candles when I couldn't hold my excitement any longer.

"Sarah, I'm so excited about Steve's visit tomorrow," I said. "I think he and Leanne have something important to tell me and that's the purpose of the visit."

"You think maybe he might be moving in with Leanne?" Sarah asked.

"Oh, I don't think so. Steve doesn't do the living together thing. He told me once that he thought if you felt strong enough about someone to want to live with them, then you should be willing to make a lifelong commitment. Even though Steve's my baby brother, he has always watched over me. He was there for me to lean on during my darker moments. He's my rock, but it's time for him to be happy. He deserves it."

I continued jabbering away. "Once, Steve got quite serious about one girl. I thought that my baby brother was finally going to get married. Next thing I knew he and this girl had broken up. The only reason he gave for the break up was that she liked to party and didn't want to settle down. After that, I figured that marriage and children were more important to him than he outwardly showed. Steve loves children."

Sarah usually did all the talking when we got together, but not this time. I tend to babble endlessly whenever I'm excited. Sarah stopped what she was doing and sat on a chair beside a table where a big basket display sat filled with cooking accessories.

She had put the table and chair in the store because she found that the older shoppers needed a place to rest. They would thumb through the gadgets and buy items they hadn't planned on and the store's sales increased.

Sarah's face turned more serious. Her eyebrows furrowed as she said, "Stephanie, I know your brother is a good guy, but I think men are different. It's not natural for them to want to get married. If they do, it's not the same as when women get married."

Her eyes had a hint of tears forming and her voice became distant as if she were talking to herself. "I think men see their wives more like business partners. They expect a wife to focus on only them. Like it's a wife's duty to help build her husband's career."

She stopped abruptly as if she just became fully conscious of the subject of our conversation. She smiled sheepishly and looked at me. "Maybe, that's why Steve hasn't found someone.

Perhaps, his girlfriends weren't into his career. Men may like the idea of children, but it's in their nature to think of themselves first. A family only complicates things for men."

I'd never heard Sarah talk so negatively. How could she have such a view of marriage? I knew she and Tony had been having trouble, but it was as if she had turned completely against men. All men.

"Sarah, my brother isn't like that. He has been hurt in the past by women who were only out for a good time. When he realized they didn't want anything permanent, he got so depressed."

I searched for something good to point out to her, something in her life that could change her pessimistic view. "Think about it. Tony's a man and he's not that way," I said. "He loves you and the girls. Sure, things change when you have kids—it's hard to keep up the romance. Even without children, everyday life takes over. It never stays the same as when people are dating."

"I'm sorry," Sarah said. Her attitude was steadfast. "I know your brother is a good guy. I didn't mean to say he was unfeeling." She shrugged and added in a patronizing way. "I'm sure Steve is different, Stephanie. However, most men aren't like your brother. I know Tony's first thoughts are himself, then his job, then the girls, and somewhere after that . . . me."

I had to say something.

"You're not last. Tony loves you," I argued. "Men have a lot of stress. He's probably just going through a rough time, that's all. Even though women now have careers, men still are ultimately responsible for taking care of their family. That must be a heavy burden."

I wasn't sure if my words were correct. Maybe Sarah's bleakness was due to a breakup with her and "Mr. Wonderful." On the other hand, if her rendezvous in Milledgeville were her way to cope with her failing marriage, then no words of encouragement would help.

"Yes, I guess you're right," she said, forcing a smile. "So, do you think Steve and Leanne are going to get married?"

Before I could answer, the bell over the front door jingled.

"Yoo-hoo, anyone here," Gladys called out. Then we heard the church bells ringing in the distance.

"Guess church is out," we said in unison.

A Ghost Comes to Dinner

I woke up early. The birds were singing outside and the sunlight warmed my bed as I laid there making a mental list of the things I had to do before my brother and Leanne arrived. Leanne had called last night to say they'd be over around three-thirty.

I think I'll make lasagna. That way I can put it in the oven, let it cook and we can talk without me having to be in the kitchen, cooking over a hot stove.

I hopped out of bed. I still had to clean the house and shop for groceries. I went to my dresser and pulled out my comfortable blue pants. The ones that I wore that first night I drove into town. It seems like a lifetime ago.

I looked down at the pants in my hand with the orange and yellow paint stains and tossed them on the bed. Opening the drawer again, I grabbed a pair of jeans and slipped them on, then I pulled on a yellow sweatshirt. After putting on some shoes, I headed toward the door and paused to look back at the pants on the bed. I grabbed them, and started out of the bedroom pausing only momentarily at the waste can to throw the pants away. Without missing a beat, I moved forward, it was time to start a fresh new day.

A FEW HOURS LATER

The aroma of freshly cooked sauce spilled into the living room, filling the air with the fragrances of spicy Italian sausage, sweet onion, and a hint of fresh basil. The big roasting pan full of several layers of noodles and all the other layers of ingredients for my homemade lasagna sat next to the sink, waiting for the precise time to go into the oven.

There was enough to feed an army because it's impossible to make a little bit of lasagna. That was okay, I could always freeze what we didn't eat. Lasagna is always better the second time around, anyway.

The table in the formal dining room was set. I'd unpacked the dishes my mother-in-law gave Daniel and me the first Christmas after we were married. My grandmother's lace tablecloth gave the perfect finishing touch. Everything looked perfect.

By ten after three, everything was in place. Twenty minutes would give me enough time to review the dates, letters, and things about Mabel and Jacob before Steve and Leanne arrived. All of the Brewer documents lay on the kitchen table in neat, organized stacks so I wouldn't forget anything. Betsy would've been proud if she'd seen it. She couldn't have done it any better herself. Everything was in flawless order.

Maybe I'm wrong to tell Leanne today about the unopened letters from Jacob. I don't want to spoil their announcement.

Poor Mabel and Jacob, they never had a chance for happiness. I couldn't be sure how Leanne would react to the letters. She might think that I was snooping into her business, the way Clarence thought. I couldn't change things now. Everything was already set in motion. Steve and Leanne knew I wanted to talk to them about what I'd found.

Why was it that people always feel they know what's best for others? I thought about the pain brought by Cain's interference between his daughter and Jacob. Even if the intentions are good, nothing good ever comes from imposing your will on others.

There was a good chance that Leanne would be mad about my search. Leanne and Steve might not understand why I started probing into the Brewers' history and Jacob's life. I didn't even fully understand it. It had been as if some unknown reason, a force, kept me looking for answers.

What if Steve and Leanne decide to stop talking to me? I was starting to panic when I heard my brother's voice.

"Hello, Steph. We're here." Then Steve and Leanne called through the front screen door in unison. "Something sure smells good."

They were here and no matter what doubts I had, there was no turning back.

"I'm coming," I yelled as I headed to the front door. "Come in. I was just straightening up a couple of things in the kitchen."

I got to the middle of the living room as they were coming into the house. Steve looked great, as usual. He wore black jeans and a blue shirt that made his blue eyes even more intense. My brother looked like a leading man in the movies. Leanne wore a cream blouse with a crocheted rust-colored vest and brown jeans. Her eyes sparkled with delight. She held a basket of yellow spider mums.

"These are for you," she said, as she handed the flowers to me and flashed a brilliant, Farrah Fawcett smile. "I know I probably should've bought poinsettias, but these were so cheerful."

"Thank you. You didn't need to bring flowers, it's not anything special, just a family dinner," I said, as I gave Steve a wink.

"Well, I told Leanne that we don't need to follow any kind of dinner invitation etiquette, but she insisted."

"I wasn't following any rule," she said. She turned to Steve, giggled, and said, "Now give her what *you* bought, mister smarty pants."

"Oh, yeah. Here." Steve thrust a bottle of champagne at me that he'd been holding. "You need to chill it."

"Champagne. Well, well, do we have something to celebrate?"

"After dinner, Steph. First, it's your turn. You said you had things you found in the house that you wanted to show us. Unless dinner is ready."

"No, dinner still needs to cook," I answered.

"Okay then, are we going to see what the old lady left behind? Or did her spirit bring it to you in the middle of the night?" Steve said followed by a ghostly whooo-ing sound and widening of his eyes.

"Stop," Leanne said pushing at his arm. "Your sister said she had something important to show us. Don't make fun."

Yep, I'm committed to showing them now, that's for sure. But then, maybe I shouldn't use that word, committed, not in this house.

"Yes, Steve that's terrible," I said shaking my finger in disapproval. "You should show some respect for Miss Brewer. She was a good person from everything I've found. She didn't deserve the things that happened to her.

"Come into the kitchen, I'll put the lasagna in the oven. That will give us time to discuss what I've found."

We sat at the table while I explained how I had stumbled onto Cain's journal, the Bible, and the rest of the papers.

"Leanne, for some reason I felt a connection to Miss Brewer," I explained. I wanted Leanne to understand why I had dug into the Brewers' past. I wanted her to know the young Mabel, the way her Uncle Jacob would've known her.

"When I first saw this house and the garden, I felt a duty to Mabel's memory. Everyone had stories about the house and family. Many in town knew Mabel, but it seemed no one was close to her. She was isolated, alone, and I felt the sadness that surrounded her. Maybe that's why I felt a bond to her."

I paused and looked directly at Leanne. "I know Steve told you about my losing Lily. Family and friends, at least, the few friends who stayed around, couldn't help with the isolation I felt. No matter how much love and support they gave me, I was alone, just like Mabel."

"I can't imagine the hurt you felt," said Leanne, softly touching my hand. "Steve loved her, too, but that can't compare to a mother's loss and what you've gone through—still go through. Steve cried when he told me about Lily, even though it's been more than a year since her death. Stephanie, you don't have to share this with me." Leanne had tears in her eyes. "Just know I'm here for you however you need me."

Hearing her words gave me the strength to believe she'd understand my probing into Mabel's past. If you listen with an open heart, you can hear someone's love. Her non-judging love must've been a conduit to Jacob's spirit, who helped guide her to Havenridge.

"Leanne, I think there are *other* reasons why I've been connected to Mabel Brewer. And it's important for you to hear them because they're linked to you."

I continued with my story. "When I moved into this house, I started getting the garden back in order. I felt that Mabel must've loved the garden because it had elaborate flowerbeds designed all around the house. They were overgrown with weeds and littered with dead plants. Still, at one time, they must've been beautiful. After I planted some bushes and the flowerbeds started to resemble a garden, again, it made me happy. I felt inspired to pack away some things related to Lily, and that's when I found these things in a box."

We went through the letters and I told her how Betsy and I had not opened Jacob's letters until a week ago. That's when Betsy made the connection to Leanne's uncle.

Leanne said that she had letters from her uncle Jacob indicating he was traveling to find work and planned to come back to Havenridge for his bride-to-be. The letters never gave his sweetheart's name, that's why Leanne hit a dead end and figured her search was hopeless.

As I presented each of her uncle Jacob's letters, Leanne's questions of what happened to her wandering uncle's bride-to-be were answered. Leanne was so glad I'd found the letters and said her uncle's spirit would now be comforted by the fact that his remaining family would have the truth about his love for Mabel.

"I've never understood why I would feel at peace anytime I drove past this property," Leanne said. "I knew I wanted to buy a house and make Havenridge my home. However, the only house for sale then was the one on the hill. At least it was near this one. Any others for sale were a distance away and didn't feel right. When all of Betsy's efforts to find something out about my uncle Jacob came up empty, I just figured I wasn't supposed to find out anything. Stephanie, with what you found, I think my uncle and Mabel can now be at peace."

We talked some more and decided that what led both of us must have been spirit-driven. Then the oven timer went off and we moved to the dining room, bringing serving bowls and platters. The house filled with laughter and conversation as we ate.

After tasting everything Steve said, "Stephanie, you amaze me. Not only do I have a beautiful sister, but she also knows how to cook a damn good meal." It may have sounded like a flowery compliment from anyone else, but my brother always speaks from his heart.

Everything *was* perfect. After dinner, we cleared the table and the three of us worked together cleaning up the kitchen. As Leanne put the last plate away and I dried my hands, Steve wrapped his arms around us and said, "I believe the champagne is chilled by now."

"We brought some champagne flutes," Leanne added. "They're on the porch in a bag. I'll go get them."

"Steph, everything is done here," Steve said. "Why don't you go sit down in the living room? I'll open the champagne."

I left to go sit in the living room. Looking around, I thought, *one short year and so much is different. This feels like my home now. I think Mabel has turned it over to me.*

Leanne hurried in from the porch and smiled as she went to join Steve in the kitchen.

The Brewer house was built more than a hundred years ago, still, I knew that it must have been a happy home once, filled with hopes and dreams. I heard the pop of the bottle and then Leanne and Steve's laugher.

Happiness has finally been restored to this grand house.

Leanne and Steve walked in carrying three glasses filled with the sparkling wine.

"We have the bubbly," they both said with a mischievous giggle and a twinkle in their eyes.

After Steve gave me a glass, he took Leanne's hand. He raised his glass and said, "Steph, may I present to you, my bride-to-be. Leanne has agreed to be my wife. We're planning to be married this spring and we're hoping we can have a garden wedding here at your new home."

The Christmas Party

Steve and Leanne's announcement kept playing in my mind as I drove to the store. Last night's events had been so perfect; it could've been a scene out of the movies. I could hardly wait to tell Sarah about it. I got to the store a few minutes before her, so I opened up, got the money drawer counted, and even got the last box of Christmas ornaments priced and put out. I was putting the empty packing box in the back room when Sarah walked in.

"Oh, I didn't expect to see you here already. Am I late?" Sarah asked. As she put her things down and hung up her coat. "How did it go with your brother last night?"

"Great and no, you're not late. I just woke up early. I got the money drawer out and finished putting the last of the Christmas ornaments on the shelves. Oh yeah, and I already made the coffee. Why don't you get a cup? Maybe before our first customer comes in I can tell you about last night. I'll meet you at the small table out front."

A few minutes later Sarah joined me, carrying two cups.

"We better take advantage of this time and sit while we can," Sarah said as she placed a steaming cup of coffee in front of me. "Yesterday I was busy all day. You wouldn't think it would be possible in a small town. Of course, not everyone who came in bought something, but just about everybody in town stopped by to inform me of their day's schedule." She blew a cooling breath on her hot coffee then said, "Now, tell me about what happened last night."

I told her of the plans for the spring wedding at my home. Remembering how depressed she seemed to be on Sunday, I kept my excitement toned down. I tried to involve her in the planning. Knowing what a gourmet cook she was, I asked if she could teach me some of her specialty dishes to serve for the reception. I'd need all the help I could get and maybe it would bring back happy memories of earlier times of her marriage.

"Of course, I'll help," Sarah said. "You know how much I like to cook. You can come to my house for some lessons. That way Tony won't interrogate me about where I'm going if I were to come to your house."

It was painful to see Sarah so negative, although she attempted to mask it by acting enthusiastic about the wedding. I tried to suppress my happiness but it only made matters worse. The tension in the air was obvious. I decided to come right out and say something.

"Sarah, we're friends, I want to help. I can tell something is wrong. I'm not trying to meddle, but sometimes it helps to talk."

"No, there's nothing wrong," she said, forcing a smile. However, it proved to be harder than she could bear. Her lips started to quiver, the smile left her face, and then, she broke down crying. "I don't know what's wrong," she sputtered. "Tony's so distant. He's angry all the time, at least, with me." Between sobs, she added, "I used to be hurt because he acted indifferent toward me as if our marriage was just a comfortable habit for him. And now, I'm home more. I'm trying so hard, I haven't gone on any shopping trips to Milledgeville in months."

She dabbed her tears. "Now it's like he's stopped loving me. Christmas is only a couple of weeks away. I just don't know how we'll get through the day. His parents don't live close so we won't be going over to see them. After the girls open their toys, they'll go off to play with them. We'll be stuck for hours alone together. How we'll get through that long day, I just don't know."

There had to be something I could do for her. Christmas is the one day of the year that should be enjoyable. Without any tension or stress.

"Maybe I can help," I said. "I'm alone in that big house. I know Steve and Leanne will come over for a little while, but that won't fill my day. Why don't I have a Christmas Day party? You, Tony and the girls can come. I know Betsy and Joe are alone, maybe they can come and Steve and Leanne. It'll be fun. If there's a party planned for later, Steve can be with Leanne alone in the morning, and he won't feel guilty about not spending the whole day with poor little old me."

Sarah's smile returned and a look of relief came over her face. Maybe a Christmas party could help them get past this awkward time. It was obvious with what Sarah had said that her fling with Mister Wonderful had ended. Maybe she and Tony could somehow re-kindle their relationship. The rest of the day flew by as we helped customers. Between sales, we discussed food for Christmas Day. I thought it would work out well for me because it could be kind of a mini dry run for hosting a house full of wedding guests.

CHRISTMAS DAY

The scent of apple cider with butter and cinnamon simmering on the stove filled the house with an inviting aroma. I decided to serve a cold buffet, that way everyone could come whenever it was convenient and leave anytime. I prepared a ham, macaroni salad, deviled eggs, green and kidney bean salad, and rolls. I had made a tray of Christmas cookies, too. Green cut out Christmas trees and sugary snowmen with candy eyes and raisin buttons down their bellies. They gave the festive touch to complete the table.

I'll have food leftover until the end of January, I thought. I surveyed the table of overfilled bowls of food and knew that Sarah and Betsy would bring some food, even though I told them it wasn't necessary. I was glad to have everyone coming even though the reason for the party started because of poor Sarah feeling so bad.

I looked around the house and said, "Mabel, I hope you like what I've done with your house. And I hope you won't mind but from now on I'll be calling it my home. Stephanie's home. Sounds good, don't you think?"

At that moment, I heard the doorbell ring. Upon opening the door, I saw Betsy and Joe kissing. "Well, hello, you two."

"Oh, Merry Christmas, Stephanie," Betsy said as she turned bright red. Joe just grinned and pointed above his head. "It's your fault—mistletoe."

"Well, you're certainly right, Joe. You two come in, that is if you're done necking," I said. "Merry Christmas, Betsy. What do you have? I told you not to go to any trouble cooking something."

"It wasn't any trouble. You know idle hands are the devil's workshop. They're homemade. One is cherry and one is mincemeat."

"Betsy makes the best pies," Joe chirped in.

As we were making room for the pies on the table, the doorbell rang again. The door opened before I got there and Steve and Leanne entered. Leanne had the deepest red poinsettia plant in one arm and three wrapped gifts under her other arm. Steve was carrying a white poinsettia and a bottle of wine.

"Sarah just drove up," Steve said.

Everyone was wishing each other a happy holiday and hanging up coats when Sarah came in with a big bowl in her hands.

"Sarah, where's Tony and the girls?" I asked.

"I brought my fried chicken. Oh, Stephanie, the house is decorated beautifully," she said looking around, before heading to the dining room table without answering my question. As we made space for the chicken, she turned to me.

"Tony's bringing the girls in *his* car," she whispered. "He said he thought we should drive separately, in case I wanted to party and drink too much. That way he could take the girls home. Stephanie, he can be so mean at times. This morning he made me feel like I was an intruder when the girls were opening their presents." She gave a nervous look over her shoulder at the chattering guests. "Don't say anything to Betsy and Joe. I don't think Tony will act badly in front of anyone."

Tony and the girls arrived shortly afterward. The rest of the day was filled with little girls' giggles, Christmas music, good food, and good cheer. The joy was tempered only by what I reluctantly feared was ahead in Sarah's future. Around eleven o'clock everyone piled out of the house, exchanging hugs and smiles. When Sarah hugged me goodbye, she whispered in my ear, "Thanks, Stephanie, I wouldn't have made it through the day without you."

Changed

I don't know whether there was one particular moment I could mark when my life had changed, leaving me at peace and happy again. I think, instead, it was a slow metamorphosis. The change was a combination of growth through marked days on the calendar and my reconnection with people. I know Clarence, Betsy, Sarah and even Gladys coming into my life were a big part of the change. Perhaps Mabel's spirit instigated it, causing a domino effect.

All I knew was once I used to wake up dreading each day, then one day; I woke up happy and looking forward to a brand new day. I found myself excited about the future, one that held a springtime wedding for my brother. My heart will always have an empty space left from losing my Lily, and it aches, but the ache had waned. The love of new friends, a future sister-in-law, and perhaps, a man somewhere down the road for me helps fill the emptiness.

MORNING 8:50

I'd been so busy helping Leanne with wedding plans that I'd been late for work every day last week. I was determined to get there early today. I pulled into the store's back parking lot and saw Sarah's car.

I wonder why Sarah's here.

We had gone back to our regular shifts once the holiday season ended and she wasn't due in until two-thirty. I unlocked the back door, stepped in, and noticed all the lights were still off.

"Sarah, it's me. What are you doing here? You're not due in until this afternoon." I put my things down and went to turn on the lights.

"Did you make coffee?"

Silence.

"Sarah?"

I walked to the front of the store and saw her sitting behind the counter facing the front window with her back to me.

"Sarah, why are you sitting in the dark?"

She didn't turn around or even mutter an answer.

"Sarah. What are you" As I moved closer, I saw it.

In her hand.

A gun.

I could see the side of Sarah's face, tear-stained and frozen like a mannequin with no visible expression, just staring out the window. My heart raced but my body stood paralyzed with fear.

What happened? Where did she get a gun? The questions spun in my mind, making me dizzy. I felt nauseated. *What should I say?*

Whatever I said, I had to choose my words very carefully.

"Sarah, what's going on?"

I didn't want to push her over the edge. Obviously, on the edge is exactly where she was, I knew that instantly after seeing her, even before I noticed the gun.

Her hand was wrapped tightly around the gun handle, the hammer pulled back with her finger posed ready on the trigger. Her hand rested on the counter on top of a letter. I couldn't see it well enough to read what it said, nor could I identify the handwriting.

In front of her sat a picture of her girls. Michelle was in a lavender dress with daisies in her hair. Abby wore a yellow dress and had lavender and yellow bows in her hair.

"I've lost them. They're both gone," Sarah said blankly.

My mind spun with a myriad of possibilities. When Lily died, I remember repeating to Steve, "I've lost her, I've lost her." Over, and over again, I couldn't stop saying it, as if by saying it out loud I could wake myself up from an evil nightmare.

Had there been an accident? Were the girls dead? How could life be so cruel? What could I say to convince Sarah to go on living?

"What do you mean? Lost who, Sarah? How?"

"I've lost Michelle and Abby. Tony took them away."

I tried to absorb her words. "Tony took them away?"

"I've ruined everything. I was just so lonely."

Tony must've found out about her Monday rendezvous with her Mister Wonderful. But how? Sarah had said he'd been asking a lot of questions about her comings and goings lately.

"We'll figure it out," I said. "You'll get them back. We'll find a way to fix it."

My only focus was to buy time and stall her. I knew I had to keep her talking and forget about using the gun. Maybe I could convince her to give it to me.

"Tony only cared about his work, how much money he made, or a new car he just bought. He didn't ever think about me."

Her voice was void of emotion. Almost . . . mechanical sounding. "He never thought I was good enough. I think he thought I was lazy or stupid because I didn't care about making a lot of money."

She spoke as if she was alone, talking to herself.

"He always wanted more. He was mad at me for not caring about things and being content to be home with the girls and not work. That's why I bought the store, so I could make him happy and still be there for the girls. I tried to show him I could be a success, even though I didn't finish college."

Desperate to get her mind off the girls not being with her I replied, "Sarah, you *are* successful. Tony knows that, and he knows you're a good mother. He'll be back."

If she felt she caused Tony to take the girls away and she would never see them again, she might use the gun to punish herself.

"I didn't care about college. I suppose that's another reason he thought I was lazy. Now he's taken the girls. He never even wanted to have children. That's what he told me once. I guess I'm to blame for that, too."

"Sarah, look at me. We can talk this over. We'll find an answer, but you need to give me the gun."

"He took them." She kept on talking, as if I wasn't there, as if she didn't hear me. "I woke up and found the note. The girls won't understand. They're going to be afraid. They're going to think I don't love them."

"Sarah, you have to give me the gun!"

"Gun?" She looked down at her hand. "Oh yeah, Tony bought it when we moved here. At first, I was home alone with the girls. He traveled out of town for months getting the business off the ground. I didn't want a gun in the house with the children. But Tony insisted. Tony *always* insists. He's always right." She paused and pulled the gun to her chest, holding it there tight with both hands. "No Stephanie, I need the gun now."

"No, you don't. If you use it, Tony will have to tell the girls, and you wouldn't want that."

She kept saying in a low voice that everything was ruined because of her and that she was all alone. Then she started to cry again.

"Nobody will understand," she said through sobs. "Betsy is the only one that I could ever count on. She never judged me. She helped me when I wanted to go to meet David. The funny thing was Betsy is the one who's the most in love with her husband. She could never think of cheating on him. She didn't understand about David, but she didn't think I was bad."

I wasn't getting through to her. She looked down at the gun and brought it up slowly toward her head. Her hand shook as she sobbed, hysterically. That's when I realized what Sarah had said. *Betsy understood!*

"Wait! We need to call Betsy. Sarah, you said she helped you. Betsy will know what to do."

Sarah paused.

"Can I call her?" I asked.

I hated to put Betsy in the middle of this, but I hadn't said anything right so far. Nothing was getting through to her.

Hearing Betsy's name, Sarah seemed to come out of her trance-like state. A look of relief came over her face. She lowered the gun and wiped away her tears with her other hand.

"Yes, call Betsy," Sarah said with a hint of hope in her voice. "She will know what to do. Michelle and Abby have never been away from me before. Michelle will be afraid. Abby will probably just think she's on an adventure. Maybe Betsy will know what to do . . . before it's too late."

I slowly walked over to the phone, afraid that if I rushed, it might spook her. I picked up the phone, and with my hand shaking, I dialed Betsy's number.

"Hello," Betsy answered.

Forcing back my tears I said, "Betsy, it's Stephanie. Sarah and I need you at the store. Can you come right now? It's important."

The Melt Down

The silence wrapped around us, threatening to suffocate any hope for Sarah. I stood next to the phone, cemented in place, waiting for Betsy. Sarah sat a few feet away on the stool, keeping a white knuckle-hold on the gun.

A minute or two passed before I drummed up the courage to speak. "Sarah, can I get the other stool and bring it there to sit beside you?"

I didn't want to scare her with any sudden moves. I wanted her to feel like she had control of something in her life. I hoped it would encourage her to accept options—other than pulling the trigger.

"Okay. But Stephanie, I don't want to talk about it. Not until Betsy gets here."

"That's fine, we'll just sit together. Remember, you're not facing this alone. Betsy and I will always be here for you. We'll find a solution."

Once again, I found myself following my brother's lead, depending on his experience. He had been in a similar situation of an attempted suicide. My fear was that I might do something wrong and place Sarah in the ultimate losing position. Even at my lowest point, when I was the most depressed, I had never considered suicide.

What Steve told me about what he had learned from that night helped me now.

* * *

Steve had ridden on patrol one night with his best friend, Robert, who was a cop. The city had a program that allowed private citizens to ride-along in a police squad car during a shift on duty. That night, a code thirty-two came over the radio. Robert answered the dispatcher and turned on his flashers. He spun the car around and they took off. Robert started rapid-firing instructions to my brother, all the time speeding through the streets with lights flashing.

"When we get there try not to get in the way," he told Steve. "And don't do anything. No sudden moves and try to keep your mouth shut! If you do anything, move, speak, anything, make sure you ask if it's okay with her first. We don't want to agitate her. And, do not try to be a hero."

They came to a screeching halt in front of a small house. In the front yard, a woman stood wielding a knife and yelling, "I'm going to do it. Don't try to stop me. I'm going to cut my throat. They'll all be sorry."

The memory of my brother's story rushed into my mind and what he said about any movement could change an attempted suicide to a completed one. I have never experienced anything like that night until now, and I didn't want to push Sarah over the edge. She obviously had the same mindset as the woman with the knife. I had to go slowly and ask permission for everything before I moved, or did anything, like asking if I could call Betsy.

I stood watching her for a few seconds and then asked, "Sarah, can I pull another stool over so we can sit together?"

She looked at me blankly. I didn't know if she had heard me or if she was trying to decide if she could trust me. Trust is a scary thing to give when you feel there is no hope left. If I hadn't been so lost myself, I might have recognized how bleak she had become over the last months.

I waited.

"Okay," she said.

When is Betsy going to get here? I thought. I wished there had been a way to warn Betsy what she was going to be walking into, but Sarah had been listening when I was on the phone.

A continual dull thumping echoed in my ears. The thunderous beat got louder. At first, I thought it was the clock on the wall striking a murderous countdown, and then I realized the pounding came from inside of me. Instinctively my body reaction of *fight or flight* was kicking into place. My heartbeat pounded and my chest felt as if it were about to explode.

We waited for ten minutes, but it felt like hours. Then I heard the back door open.

"Hello, Stephanie . . . Sarah."

Finally, Betsy's here. "Yes," I called out. I turned to Sarah. "Sarah, I'm going to go get Betsy. Okay?"

"All right, but I'm staying here," she said. As I slid off the stool, she grabbed my arm. "Wait, I was thinking, I don't think even Betsy's going to be able to fix this."

Then her eyes lost the glimmer of hope that had been there after I had suggested calling Betsy. She turned and stared out the front window where the other shop owners were opening up for business.

"It will be all right, Sarah. Don't do anything. I'll be right back with Betsy."

I quickly headed to the back and met Betsy at the stockroom door.

"Stephanie."

197

"Shhhh! Betsy, I'm sorry, I didn't know what else to do. Sarah was so distraught. All she kept saying was the girls were gone and she had lost them."

"Oh my God, no. I knew something was wrong when I heard your voice." Betsy started to move forward and I stopped her.

"Betsy, wait. Sarah has a gun. I couldn't get her to give it to me. She said she needs it. Tony—"

"It's okay Stephanie, we'll help her," Betsy said as she pushed past me. "Sarah, it's Betsy, I'm here."

"Betsy, I don't know what I'll do," Sarah called out.

Betsy hurried toward Sarah. I followed her and stopped a step behind, not wanting Sarah to feel that we were rushing her.

Let Betsy talk to her. She listens to Betsy. Betsy can fix it. I recited the words over in my mind like a prayer. *Betsy can fix it.*

When Betsy saw Sarah, her eyes began to tear up. She looked gently at Sarah and then she looked over to the counter at the pictures of the girls. She looked back at Sarah, and asked, "Michelle and Abby . . . . *both* girls? What happened?"

"Oh Betsy, I've lost them. What am I going to do? I can't live without them. Tony took them away. He says he wants a divorce and he's going to raise them," Sarah said with tears streaming down her face.

Betsy's eyes widened and her face stiffened. The muscles in her neck bulged. Then her eyes narrowed with a fury in them that I've never seen before. She lunged toward Sarah, grabbing the gun with her left hand, trying furiously to wrestle it away. They both held tight to the gun. Betsy's right hand flung back, then down with such speed that I felt a rush of air pass by my face. The sound of the slap across Sarah's face pierced the once quiet room.

I took a step forward. "Betsy, no! Stop," I cried out.

Betsy's hand propelled back and down again, connecting with Sarah's skin. "How dare you! How dare you even think of leaving those beautiful girls motherless," Betsy screeched. Slapping over, over, and over again.

"Betsy, I'm sorry," Sarah cried. "I'm, I'm sorry."

"Stop," I begged. Our frantic cries continued over top of each others' voices.

"No Betsy."

"How dare you."

"I'm sorry."

"Stop it."

Our pleas were muffled by sounds of the slaps.

"How dare you. How dare you," Betsy kept repeating between blows.

Then the deafening *bang,* followed by sounds of glass shattering, and Sarah's final scream.

Sarah let go of her grip on the gun and fell on the counter sobbing.

Betsy and I froze for a second. Betsy stood with the gun in her hand. She looked at me and then rushed toward the back of the store. I looked to my left and saw broken glass everywhere. Half of the glass shelves that once held holiday clearance and stemware lay scattered in pieces on the floor. The bottom shelf still attached to the wall had one goblet on its side, knocked over from the eruption and cascading shelves. The stemmed glass rolled toward the edge, lingered, teetering for a moment, and then crashed to the floor on top of the pile of shards of broken glass. I looked at Sarah crying and moved toward her, but stopped when I heard the hammering at the front door.

"Sarah . . . Stephanie, open the door. Are you all right?" The neighboring shop owners called frantically from outside. I went to the door, turned the lock, and opened it to a half dozen people who poured into the store. Outside, I saw more people running from across the street.

"What happened? Are you all right?" They all spoke at once. "Was that a gunshot?" They looked over to Sarah, "Sarah, are you hurt? What happened?"

Sarah lifted her head, "No I haven't been shot. I'm okay."

"Everything is fine," Betsy said from behind us. She crossed the room and continued speaking to the concerned crowd, now growing in size. "Sarah has made a mistake. Like we all have done at one time or another, no different than any of us. She's going to have to face the consequences of her actions."

Betsy turned and looked at Sarah. "No matter what they may be." She turned back to the gathering crowd and instructed them. "So, best everyone go back to whatever you were doing and don't be wagging your tongues with any gossip."

Betsy turned to Sarah and me and said, "There'll be no more keeping secrets. There's been enough of that."

She turned back to the crowd. "All of you need to remember that you're all good Christian people and Sarah's going to need our support in the days to come."

Then Betsy gently showed each person out, while thanking them for their concern. She hugged each of them and reassured them, saying "Everything will be all right." Then, she closed the door and turned the lock.

"Betsy, I'm sorry," Sarah said, wiping her eyes, "I just felt so scared that I'd never see my girls again. I didn't know what to do. I wouldn't hurt Michelle or Abby. I wouldn't ever leave them."

"I know, Sarah. I should not have hit you. We'll keep the store closed today and talk about some choices you've got for resolving things. I locked the gun in my car. I'm going to keep it for now," Betsy said with firm conviction. "Do you know where Tony went with the girls?"

"Yes, he's gone to his parent's house."

"I'll call him after we talk about what you're willing to do," Betsy said with the tenderness I recognized to be uniquely Betsy. She put her arm around Sarah and comforted her. "I'll see if he wants to try to work this out. But Sarah, whether the two of you can work this out or not, you both are those girls' parents. They will have the two of you in their lives, whether you're together or not."

"Thank you," Sarah said smiling. "You're right. Thank you, Betsy."

I went over to Sarah, hugged her, patted Betsy's hand, and said, "I'll go make some coffee for us and get a broom to sweep up the glass."

Springtime

FOUR MONTHS LATER

I opened the store, put the coffee on, and headed to the front to check the window from outside. Betsy and I had hired Eric Trenton for the new signage on the front window. He studied art in college and did artistic jobs on the side. He and his wife, Marcy, were expecting their first child by the middle of October so they needed the extra money. Eric had not finished the lettering when I left yesterday and I was eager to see it.

I went outside and turned around to face the window. As promised, he'd completed the job, and it looked perfect. I examined the hand-painted writing on the glass. It brought bittersweet feelings. In small letters, it read, "General store, gifts, teas, and books." Above that, in larger lettering read, "Stephanie & Betsy's Gathering Spot."

Even though Sarah had been thrilled that Betsy and I had bought the shop, it just didn't feel right for the store to keep the old name. The store had been Sarah's creation. She had nurtured it and it had truly been her baby, the old name belonged to Sarah.

Nevertheless, she didn't hesitate to part with the store. With the transition of new ownership, it went through a rebirth. As Sarah had changed, so did the little general store and it required a brand-new name.

With the shift in ownership, we knew we would never be able to keep the same atmosphere without Sarah as the proprietor, nor did we want to. That's what gave me the idea to add a corner where reading groups could meet. We added the book section to the store and stocked an assortment of special blends of herbal teas.

Five clubs were meeting monthly now to chat about their current reading pick and sip the fresh-brewed "tea of the month" served in English bone china teacups. April's tea of the month was Ginger Peach Black Tea.

Of course, the china teacup selection and new herbal teas increased sales for the store. The announcement of each monthly selection brought a lot of attention.

The start of the New Year bought new beginnings, fresh energy, and changes for many people of Havenridge.

As Steve and Leanne's wedding date approached, Joe offered to build a gazebo in my back yard among the magnolias. It would serve as a platform for the bride and groom to take their vows. Joe said it was his contribution to the wedding. Also, it would symbolize the friendship formed between Betsy, Joe, and me.

I never would've thought of adding a gazebo to my back yard. The design and detail flawlessly matched the house. It gave the final, finishing touch to the back yard. Joe's talent was amazing. My task of restoring the Brewer house now was complete with the gazebo and gardens flourishing to its original grandeur, my duty to Mabel fulfilled.

With only three days left until the big day, Betsy and I planned tomorrow to prepare the gazebo for the nuptials by draping white satin ribbons along the railing and attaching bows to the base of each column. On Saturday morning, the wedding day, we would add fresh magnolias.

Leanne found out Gladys had made all the wedding cakes for the brides at the church for the last fifteen years. Steve and Leanne met with her and ordered a cake with cream cheese frosting and fresh yellow roses cascading down the tiers. The top tier would hold one white magnolia with yellow ribbons instead of the traditional bride and groom.

I'd better stop daydreaming and get the mail, I thought as I stood looking at the newly painted letters on the store window.

"Yoo-hoo, Stephanie." I heard from across the street.

I turned around and there was Gladys with one hand above her head, feverishly waving. Of course, she had her white gloves on, and in her signaling hand, she grasped a lace hankie. She ran across the street with plumped bosoms bouncing with every hurried step.

"Whew. I'm glad I caught you," she said, stepping onto the sidewalk in front of me. She fanned herself with the hankie.

"Please tell your brother I've made the cakes." As she spoke, she adjusted her pearls and the eyelet lace collar on her floral spring dress. "I make them early and freeze them, and then defrost them at dawn on the day of the wedding. I ice and assemble the cakes, and do all the decorating that day, so everything is fresh. By cake cutting time, everything is picture-perfect," she said with a big grin.

Patting the sides of her face and down her neck with her hankie, she continued, "Leanne's such a sweet thing. She and Steve invited me to the wedding. They make such an adorable couple."

"Yes, they do. They seem to be a perfect match," I said.

"Oh, dear, yes. They are just as sweet as can be. And your brother, he's quite the looker. I'm so happy they invited me to the wedding. Did they tell you that little Rachael Harrison is going to sing?"

"Yes, Leanne told me." *I wouldn't call Rachael little. She's almost twenty and has a figure that would stop traffic. I guess that's an old way, thinking of the younger generation as children even after they're grown.*

"Leanne and Steve are having her sing "The Rose." Bette somebody sang it in a movie. I tried to tell them they should have Rachael sing "Oh, Promise Me" or "I love You Truly," but they insisted they wanted the new song," Gladys said, shaking her head.

Oh, yeah, I've been transported back in time, I thought. I remembered dinners at my great Aunt Edna's house. Steve, Daniel, and I had to sit at a separate table, *the kids' table.* Right up until the year Aunt Edna passed away, we had to sit at that darn card table. Even though I was twenty-seven years old and married.

"Stephanie, I'll be coming early Saturday. I need to set the cake up—you're not having the food outside, are you? The frosting will melt," Gladys said frowning.

"No. All the food will be in the house. The wedding cake and most of the food will be in the formal dining room," I reassured her. "I'll have trays of finger food throughout the house and the bar, uh—I mean the beverages will be in the eat-in part of the kitchen."

Gladys looked relieved, not noticing my slip of the tongue about the bar. Somehow, I just knew she would object to alcohol being served. However, she was too focused on the food preparation to notice.

205

A big smile came back to her face. "Oh, good. We wouldn't want to give our guests food poisoning. After I get the cake set up, you can show me what you've done to Miss Mabel's house. It had been such a grand place before she got too old to take care of it. I hope you got rid of that awful mothball smell."

"Yes, I did," I said through clenched teeth, trying to smile. "Miss Gladys, I need to get the mail and go back into the store to listen for the phone. Would you like to come in and have some tea?"

I hoped she wouldn't want any. Miss Gladys can go on talking for what feels like an eternity when she stops to chat *'just for a minute'* as she says. I already had enough of her helpful suggestions of "not wanting to poison *our guests.*" Not to mention, her concerns about the smell of mothballs.

"Oh, dear, no. It's too early for tea and I've lots to do before Saturday. I need to press my dress for the wedding and there's still the church business I must attend to," she said, waving her lace handkerchief in the air again as she walked away. "See you on Saturday, Stephanie. And don't you worry about anything. I'll be there to help you, my dear."

I'm sure you will.

"Thank you, Miss Gladys," I called back to her as she disappeared down the sidewalk. "I won't worry."

I know you'll be there, right there underfoot.

After I got the mail, I went back into the store. Thumbing through the bills and junk mail, I found a letter with the familiar handwriting from Sarah. I wondered if I should wait for Betsy before opening it. Then I saw another envelope addressed to Betsy from Sarah. I found the letter opener and slit my envelope open. I had just talked to Sarah a few nights ago on the phone. Still, she had a habit of writing late at night when she couldn't sleep.

I unfolded the letter and read:

Dear Stephanie,

I can hardly wait to see you and Betsy again. Don't worry about messing up the Swedish meatballs that you're preparing for the wedding. You can't go wrong with my recipe. Remember Betsy said the ones you made for a practice run last month tasted great.

I finished Michelle's flower girl dress two weeks ago and hemmed Abby's dress last week. I left the hemming to go as long as I could because Abby seems to grow taller by the day. I sent a picture of the girls in the dresses to Leanne. I wanted to make sure the dresses met her approval. She loved them.

Michelle and Abby have been throwing make-believe flower petals around the house for weeks.

Tony took the girls for a weeklong visit last Friday and he's bringing them back home in the morning.

I think things are going to be okay. I got a job at a small catering company since I wrote last. I usually get off work around four-thirty. Tony takes off from his work at two to pick the girls up from school. He's renting a house about two miles away from where I live. After work, I pick the girls up from Tony's and he goes back to work. He likes the arrangement because now he gets to do his father thing and still can go to all the business functions in the evenings without any guilt.

The divorce was finalized last week. I should get my official copy within a month. It seems strange not being married anymore, but I think we're both happier.

I'll be at your house Saturday around eleven o'clock with the girls for the wedding. Tony said he's going to come, too. He always liked you and said he wouldn't miss your only brother's wedding.

I love what wrote to me about what Betsy and you did with the store. Adding books and having ladies in for meetings sounds ideal. I'm so glad I didn't have to sell the store to anyone else.

I think everything that has happened in the past year was destiny. Each of us was moved to the correct place in life.

Love ya,

Your S.O.S. friend,

Sarah

Destiny? I don't think my losing Lily, or Betsy losing Jenny, was destiny. I can't accept the events that happen in life are part of a preset plan. Things just happen as life unfolds. We might not have control of events in life. However, we are responsible for how we handle them. Our actions, whatever they may be, can either keep us locked in the moment, or they move us forward. Although I do believe angels sometimes nudge people in the right direction.

New Beginnings

When Leanne asked me months ago to be her maid-of-honor, I feared she asked out of a sense of obligation. I remembered her saying once that I could say anything to her and she wouldn't be offended. "People put too much importance on the words said and forget they know the person's heart," she said. Even though Leanne was younger in years, she had the Wisdom of Solomon. She added, "The honesty can be heard if we listen not just with our ears, but with our hearts, too."

Heeding her word, I decided to speak frankly and I hoped she would hear my heart. I started with, "Leanne, I'm honored that you asked me to be maid-of-honor. However, I don't want you to feel obligated to ask me because I'm Steve's sister. I know this request usually goes to the bride's best friend."

I crossed my fingers hoping I wouldn't hurt her feelings.

"Stephanie, don't think I'm asking for that reason. I'm a good person, but I wouldn't ask you just because you're Steve's sister. It's too important of a request," she answered. "I did a lot of traveling before I moved to Havenridge, much like Uncle Jacob. Until I moved here, I didn't put down roots anywhere. I made friends along the way, but they weren't deep relationships. We said our goodbyes when I moved on and swore we would stay in touch, but it never happened. At first, I thought everyone was just busy with their lives when my letters weren't answered.

It didn't take long for me to realize the friends I had made were only brief acquaintances. It was different when we met, Stephanie. I felt a connection to you, even before I met Steve. I didn't understand it. I knew you weren't close to anyone. With time, I understood the magnetism I felt had importance. Now I know it had nothing to do with us becoming sisters-in-law. Friendship was our destiny."

I accepted her request that day to be her maid-of-honor and recognized our bond would last a lifetime. Leanne's friendship is completely different from what I have with Betsy or Sarah. It's quiet, steady, and always constant. We inherently know we'll always be there for each other.

After that day, Leanne made one more request to me. She asked if I'd continue researching her uncle Jacob's last six months, the time after he left Mabel, and promised to return. She wanted to fill in the gaps and get answers about his death. As I thought about it, Betsy's comment to Clarence about me writing a book about the Brewers and Havenridge's history kept playing in my mind.

When I told Leanne that I thought I wanted to write a book about Mabel and Jacob's lost love, she said without hesitation, "I think that would be wonderful. I know my uncle Jacob would be happy to have someone with a good heart, like you, tell his story. I think Mabel has been waiting for you, too."

I listen with my heart a lot now, even when I have conversations with Miss Gladys.

Shortly after I accepted to be maid-of-honor, Steve asked my consent to ask Daniel to be his best man. Even though Daniel and I were divorced, I didn't feel any betrayal of loyalty from my brother. It felt right. I called Daniel that night for the first time since I'd left Orlando to tell him to feel free to answer Steve the way he wished.

THE WEDDING DAY

Leanne and I were upstairs finishing our makeup and hair. Leanne literally glowed. I'd just finished helping secure Leanne's veil and handed the pearl necklace that had been her grandmother's to her, the something old, when we heard a knock on the bedroom door.

"Stephanie, Leanne, it's Sarah and the girls. Can we come in?"

"Yes, Sarah, come in," I said and started toward the closed door. I stopped for a moment and looked back at Leanne. "You look beautiful. My brother is lucky to have found you."

With that, the door opened and two adorable flower girls entered the room, followed by Sarah. A few minutes of hugs, and sighs and statements like; "You're the most beautiful bride ever!" and "You look so pretty" followed.

Michelle and Abby showed off their dresses by twirling around the room. One girl told us that their mommy pinned the flowers in their hair and the other chimed in that their daddy was here, too.

"When I was parking, we saw Tony's car," Sarah said. "He parked behind us."

Sarah had in her hands the two ribbon-wrapped magnolias for Leanne's hair. They would add the final touch to her veil. Sarah said that most of the guests had arrived and were outside waiting for the bride.

We fastened the medium size flowers behind each ear so they overflowed toward Leanne's temples and delicately framed her face.

"Are you ready to take the big plunge?" I asked her.

Gleaming, Leanne answered, "Absolutely."

After finishing with the pinning of the magnolias, we took a couple of last-minute photos, then I heard the doorbell ring.

"I bet that's Daniel wanting to know if you're ready," I said. "I'll be right back."

As I came down the stairs, I saw Daniel waiting at the screen door.

"Come in, Daniel."

"Hi, Stephanie. Is the bride ready?" Daniel asked. "Steve's outside waiting on the porch. Should we go to the gazebo?"

"Yes, I think it's time."

Daniel turned toward the door, stopped, and turned back. "Stephanie, you look good. Looks like things are going okay for you. Steve told me that you did a lot of the refurnishing here. This house is amazing."

"Thanks."

Daniel moved forward and then stopped again. Turning back, he hesitated. "Uh, about us. I'm sorry about how things worked out. I don't think I handled everything so well. I guess with all my *genius brains,* there are still some things I can't do. I'm sorry I failed you."

"Daniel, you did what you could. You stood by me during the investigation. You did your best but we were both hurting. Both of us were lost and needed to find our own way."

"Yes, maybe," Daniel said. He started to move but hesitated again and stood in place looking down at the floor.

I didn't want him to be stuck in the past like I had been. He was a good man and I wished only the best for him.

"We weren't right for each other," I added. "Mismatched from the start. Not like Steve and Leanne. Maybe we both will find the right person someday."

He smiled, as if to himself, and then looked at me and nodded. "I'd better get Steve to the gazebo. He's going to wear a hole in your front porch floor from all his pacing, that or pick your hanging basket of ivy down to bare stems if I'm much longer."

"Okay. I'll get the bride," I answered.

I hurried up the stairs and opened the bedroom door. Leanne looked up. I think Sarah and the girls were right, she was the most beautiful bride ever.

"Ready?" I asked.

Leanne stood up, grabbed the bouquet of magnolias and yellow roses. She took a calming breath in and then out. "Yes, I'm ready. Come on girls, it's time for new beginnings for all of us."

Notes from the Author

Chris Coad Taylor

Secrets of Havenridge was my first novel and the original was written in 2006. It has always held a special place in my heart.

When I returned to write the sequel, I realized my writing had changed and improved over the years. Therefore, I wanted to revise my first book before releasing the sequel. I set out to restructure and pump-up the mystery elements, allowing my protagonist, Stephanie Oliver, to hold onto her secrets and reasons why she fled Florida and moved to Georgia for a little longer than in the first edition.

As the title implies, there are lots of secrets. Many of the people in town hold personal and dark secrets. They are revealed slowly, chapter-by-chapter as Stephanie tries to solve a hundred-year-old mystery.

I wrote Stephanie's story in a realistic way. Her life includes tension, hopefulness, unhappy moments, excitement, and ultimately peacefulness, which brings contentment back to her life.

The Lovers at Blue Lake:
Originally, I started to research about Georgia towns because I needed a source of how Cain Brewer obtained his power and money. Instead of the obvious, cotton being his source of money and driving his story, I stumbled onto the real

town of Milledgeville and found that one of America's oldest asylums had been built there. Furthermore, the Central State Mental Hospital was still in operation! (Since then, the "asylum/mental hospital", which had many names over the years, closed in 2010.) Cain's history deepened and darkened with my discovery of the Georgia asylum and the Brewer family dynamics began to evolve with new secrets emerging as I wrote.

I traveled to Georgia to gather more information and toured the grounds of the hospital and its extensive acreages. When I visited the graveyard, I discovered the statue of the "Angel of Milledgeville" that is featured in this edition. I took the actual photograph that I used for the cover. My muse had not only been awakened, it was screaming new chapters at me.

Armed with the subject of mental health, and knowledge of archaic views held in the early 1900s, I had Cain Brewer's background forming in my mind, plus a reason he raised Mabel with an iron hand. Fear of tainted blood, insanity being passed down from generation-to-generation, then add in a small town somewhere in the Bible belt, and I had the makings of a great story, enough for one, two, or three books.

Weaving facts and real history into my fictional stories have continued to be a style of mine in all of my novels. Truth hidden in fiction, golden treasures, and research are cornerstones of my fiction. I absolutely love all of it.

In this revised edition, I included new chapters, revised old ones, and had a new cover made. For me, it feels like a brand-new book, so even if you already have read the first edition, I hope you enjoyed this revised edition as much as I loved writing it.

Both novels, *Secrets of Havenridge* and *Finding Jacob* are standalone stories. You can read all of them or just one but I hope you will want to read as many as I write.

Your Author Friend,
Chris Coad Taylor

Please leave a review of this book on Amazon.

I love to hear from my readers, what you like, and the things that intrigued you each story. Be sure to follow me on my Amazon author page http://www.amazon.com/author/chriscoadtaylor or follow me on my Facebook Author page https://www.facebook.com/chriscoadtaylorauthor so you will be first to learn about new releases, discounts and sales, and future stories.

Tell a friend and look for our books in select stores. If your favorite bookstore doesn't have one of our books, ask if they will order it for you. They make great gifts for a book lover you might know.

The following pages contain Excerpts for Book 2 of the Havenridge Mystery Novels:

AN EXCERPT FROM:

Finding Jacob©

Chris Coad Taylor

Prologue

As I watched my brother in the gazebo of my backyard preparing to pledge his love for his bride, Leann, my heart filled with joy. My entire being was at peace.

Things were so different now from two years earlier. Back then, I had thought peace would never be part of my life ever again. I had been lost and filled with despair without my daughter in my life, but it was my brother who pulled me out of the hollow that had imprisoned me.

Now, I'm content. My loneliness has been lifted. Looking at the yard filled with wedding guests, I'm happy.

Across the yard, the caterers were busy arranging food trays. The fragrance of young love once again filled the air. The old Victorian house from the Brewer estate that I bought was bright again. Bitter moments of the past faded from my mind as I imagined Mabel Brewer happily in love and sneaking out of the back door of the house to meet her lover. Once I had questioned the mystery surrounding Blue Lake and the two lovers. I thought perhaps it had been a made-up fairytale of a powerful family invented by the wild imagination of the people in town. I too had questioned if the rumors were false until I found the old letters hidden in the house.

After my brother's bride had shown me a letter written by her great uncle, it confirmed the Blue Lake lovers did exist. The letter pledged his love, saying that he would return home to his beloved Mabel, the last Brewer who had lived in the house that I now owned. The fairytale romance about Mabel Brewer was true. And my brother's bride, Leann, helped put the missing pieces together.

The conversation Leann and I had before coming downstairs to join the rest of the bridal party in the gazebo echoed in my mind. "Please help find out what happened to my uncle and why he disappeared without a trace. I need to know why he didn't return for Mabel and bring her home as he said he would in the letter." I'm still a bit in shock. My mind raced with thoughts about Mabel, Jacob, and Leann's request to solve the seventy-year-old mystery.

"Do you take this woman to be your wife?" The minister's voice pierced my rambling thoughts, pushing me back into the present. My brother's blue eyes gazed at his wife-to-be.

Focus on this moment! Today was all about new beginnings and a wedding. Old mysteries can wait, the present is about my brother and his bride pledging their love to each other forever.

The two lovers of the past needed to remain in the shadows. *Mabel and Jacob's mystery will stay unsolved for a little while longer.* I scolded myself but a chill flowed over me as if a ghost had touched my arm. Was Mabel here as another couple recites wedding vows that had been forbidden for her?

"Does anyone here hold reason that these two not be wed?" the minister said. "Speak now or forev . . . er—"

"No!" A troubled voice cried out. "No, no, no."

A hush fell over the crowd . . .

New Evidence about Hanna
(Chapter in part)

The woman was talking in circles but the crazy thing was, she had piqued my interest. All the Brewers were dead. Clarence Swain was the last person in town who knew Mabel in her younger years and he had told me everything he knew. If this woman's mother knew something else, I needed her.

"What does your mother mean, families need to know?" I asked. "What families?"

I wasn't going to get roped into trusting in false information from a well-intentioned person who believed whatever her mother told her. I had heard about the road to Hell being paved by good intentions.

"I don't know what families she's talking about but it is so very important to her." Her voice quivered. It sounded like she could be trying to camouflage the sound of crying. "My mother keeps saying she needs to 'right a wrong.' She's an old woman, Miss Oliver, and she is terrified she's going to die because someone wants to stop her from talking to you. She insists she must talk to you before it is too late."

She got me with the "terrified," not to mention that this old woman thought talking to me might stop her death, so I crumbled. "Okay, I'll talk to her. Put her on the phone."

"She won't talk on the phone. She's afraid that certain people might be listening in, and if they find out what she knows . . . . She needs your help. Now, she's even afraid to take her medicine or go to sleep. Please, can you come here? I'm begging you."

"Where in Milledgeville are you?"

"My mother is on the outskirts of town, on Sinclair Lake."

"I've got a store to run. That's a long drive. Why would anyone want to hurt your mother just to keep her from talking about the past?"

"I don't know. And frankly, I really don't care. My mother was a nurse and has taken care of others all her life. Now *she* needs help. I promised her I'd help her and convince you to come."

She sounded so desperate. I couldn't refuse. I wondered if her information could have anything to do with Jacob. I wrote down the address and agreed to drive to Milledgeville tomorrow. It was my day off. I said I'd be there before noon.

"Thank you, Miss Oliver. Your visit just may keep me from losing my mother."

End of excerpt